All Shall Suffer

Chris Rush

Acknowledgements

As always, I would firstly like to thank you, the reader, for reading my story. I hope it scares you as much as possible.

I want to thank all my family and friends for the support over the last number of years – you all know who you are and I wouldn't be here without each one of you.

Thanks to Talina Perkins for bringing my crazy book cover idea to life.

Thanks to Samantha S. Lafantasie for editing my work.

Thanks to Lisa V. Proulx for her proofreading help.

"I want to bring about an eternal darkness, and it all starts with you." Natas.

Chapter 1

"Stop! Don't go in there!" A woman shouted after her five-year-old son as he ran ahead of her towards an old, broken down, wooden fence rotting from the inside out.

Behind the fence stood an equally rundown, old house. The once cream paint had faded to a dull grey in parts. Some roofing tiles were missing, swept away by numerous storms in the past, and others lay broken and unrepaired for years. The windows were covered by net curtains stained brownish-black from lack of cleaning. The surrounding garden was heavily overgrown and full of old, rusted scrap metal and broken garden furniture.

The boy ignored her.

What child doesn't at this age? She thought as he placed his tiny fingers onto the fencing.

Looking through the fence, he saw one of the net curtains move slightly behind the glass. The only thing he could see besides the tattered, dirty curtain was the old, bony hand holding it aside and the whites of glaring eyes staring back at him. The child, of course, thought nothing. He was just curious about the world like every other child at that age. However, his mother didn't share the same curiosity.

She quickly caught up to him, grabbed him by

the arm and dragged him away from the fence. "Don't run off like that again Alan!" she instructed.

With that, the hand faded back into the darkness within the house, and the curtain dangled back into its original position.

"And stay away from that house! Do you hear me?" she added.

These words had often been spoken to Alan over the first number of years of his life.

Frank Moore was the local weirdo who stereotypically kept to himself in the dank, rundown structure resembling a house. He was an old man who every kid (and some of their parents) in the community was afraid of, and for very valid reasons. Any time he ventured outside, he wore his trademark long, green trench coat which barely reached beneath the knees of his long, slender body, an old hat, plain shirt, black pants which were tread thin at the knees and boots, or if the weather dictated green wellies. His hair was always unkempt and the large crusty wart on the left side of his nose was the first thing that anyone would notice on his face. His dirt patched hands always clung to a dog lead and the animal at the end of it never looked any better than he did. It was a very old black and white sheep dog, with rattling back legs, you could tell by the grey hair around the face and the shaking back legs when he stood still, so to speak. His hair was knotted and on some parts covered his body in patches. Sam, Jim called him, and he regularly took him for walks either really early in the morning or late at night.

Trish, Alan's mother, lived in a house with her husband Daniel Cullen at the end of the road. It was a small row of ten country houses in a cul-de-sac about one and one half miles away from the nearest town, Arklow. The road itself was narrow with barely enough room for a car to pass along it, Frank's house stood at the road entrance to the cul-de-sac, so no matter what, everyone had to pass by it to get in or out.

Frank lived with his wife Stephanie, a small lady, and in her later years became hunched over due to chronic arthritis and various other ailments over her lifetime. Her face was surprisingly smooth for her age, it housed dentures and she had long white hair down to her skinny waist which she use to always tie into a plat. She wore various kinds of gold rings on all fingers and thumbs and would never be without her lucky rabbit's foot keyring, which she made herself.

Long before Alan was born, Trish and her friends use to call Stephanie scary Steph. Mainly because she use to practice some palm reading, fortune telling, and she regularly held private ceremonies. People who lived in the area claimed she could contact and talk to the dead.

Once, when Trish was fourteen years old, she and her two friends, Laura and Rachel, snuck over to the house when Stephanie was performing one of her *contact* sessions with the deceased. Laura was just as giddy and curious as Trish, she had long dark hair, brown eyes and a skinny frame. She always wore huge earrings that always looked ridiculous on either side of her face. Rachel was the *sensible* one so to speak. She had a mass of curly brown hair, a face covered in freckles and oversized glasses concealing her tiny face.

"We should go back," Rachel whispered as they walked up the moonlit road towards the dank house, which would be the perfect place for the dead to haunt if they hadn't crossed over to the other side.

The night was calm and silent, and as they edged closer to the entrance, they could see a light on in one room, no doubt where Frank watched some TV. The flickering light cast from candles bounced off the red window curtains in the other room were Stephanie was with one or two *believers*.

"We'll just take a peek, that's all," Laura said.

"Okay two minutes and that's it," Rachel anxiously replied.

They reached the edge of the wooden fence, which stood a little prouder back then, and then climbed over it. Their feet were met by the soft, wet, long grass on the other side. They crept through the lawn using the moonlight as best they could to prevent themselves tripping and landing face down in dog shit. They continued as quietly as they could towards the window containing the red curtains, hoping not to alert the dog that resided inside with the spine-chilling couple.

The three girls reached the window safely. Rachel stayed behind the shoulders of Trish and Laura who wrestled each other for the perfect view through the tiny break between the curtains.

"Hang on I'll let you look next," Trish whispered forcing herself into position.

"Hurry up then." Laura sighed.

Trish held her breath to prevent the glass fogging up and peered through the window. Inside the room, four people including Stephanie, another two women, and one man, all in their late fifties or early sixties. They were all sitting at a circular table. Steph sat on one side facing the others. Trish didn't recognise any of the other participants; they all had wrinkled faces like a road map. The man was bulky and donned glasses and a tweed shirt with the buttons barely holding the fabric around his big frame. A tiny woman sat to his right and wore a flowery dress and had dyed, broken blonde hair which didn't suit her age. The other woman was of average build and wore a white blouse with a red cardigan. She had grey locks of hair which were tied neatly into a ponytail.

Numerous candles lit the room. There were multi-coloured crystals scattered all over the table in front of the group. Incense burned in the corner of the room, whilst its fumes danced their way around the people within it. Stephanie shuffled tarot cards through her hands. She spread them out on the table and then tilted her head back towards the dull ceiling and began mumbling. The inquisitive girl found it hard to hear them through the window.

"Let me see," Laura demanded, almost giving

themselves away.

"Ssshhh!" Trish shoved Laura then turned back towards the window. Everyone was talking. Trish listened attentively and finally understood the chants inside.

"Come to us! Be with us!" Stephanie groaned out her words.

"Visit us! Stay with us!" the others chanted.

Trish couldn't take her tense, curious eyes off the activity within the room. About twenty seconds passed, and the chanting became louder. Steph continued to stare at the ceiling.

The candles flickered, and for a moment, Trish could have swore she saw something or someone move within the corner of the room. She didn't have time to think about or examine it.

Stephanie lowered her head and then glared towards the window the girls were standing behind. She looked straight at Trish with eyes that were pure white whilst they rolled back in her head, she then smiled at Trish and said, "We're not alone!"

Trish ducked underneath the windowsill, however she knew that she had been caught out.

"Great. They saw you didn't they?" Rachel said in a panicked voice. She tugged on Laura's shoulder. "We should go!"

"Ssshhh!" Every muscle tensed in Trish's body. *Why don't you make some more noise?*

Trish inhaled a deep breath and peeked over the battered, mouldy concrete into the room, but by then, everyone was gone from the table, as the light incense smoke dangled precariously in the air.

"Okay let's go!" she uttered, turning from the window and walked—almost ran—away trying to stay as crouched as possible.

When they reached the fence they all jumped it as quickly as they could. Once on the *safe* side of the Moore's property, Trish turned back towards the house. She witnessed Steph's pitch black shadow standing in the doorway glaring at the three girls. For a moment, an uncomfortable feeling overcame Trish. Stephanie didn't shout at them, didn't wave her hands angrily at them, she didn't even move. She just observed them leaving her property.

"What's she doing?" Laura said, gasping out her words.

"I don't know." Trish shrugged, panting for breath.

"I don't care what she is doing. We shouldn't have done that, I'm going home!" Rachael said.

"Me too," Laura added.

Trish looked back towards the house finding Stephanie had returned behind the door to the forbidden house.

"Okay, I'll give you guys a ring later," Trish said while trying to come to terms with the weird events she beheld.

Trish burst through the front door of her house and the first thing that hit her was the smell of her mother's home made cooking. Bread and scones, to be exact.

"Did you have a nice time at Laura's?" her mother asked while balancing the warm cooking tray in one towel-covered hand and shutting the oven door with the other.

"Yeah, we just chilled out and watched some TV," Trish replied. She had fed her mother the old *"I'm going over to my friend's house for a while"* story.

Trish's mother, Bridgett, was in her mid-fifties and still looked extremely good looking for her age. Peter, Trish's father, was carrying out his usual weekly routine of having a pint or five in the local pub.

"Try one of these, let me know what you think?" Bridgett said slicing open a soft, fluffy scone and spreading butter along it which melted instantly. Trish sat at the kitchen table while her mother passed Trish her snack. She bit into it and said, "Delicious!"

Her mother smiled and began preparing another batch.

Meanwhile Trish went to her room, climbing the stairs, the image of *Scary Steph* standing within the shadows of the doorway still haunted her. Flicking on the bedroom light, she went over and lay down on her tossed bed. Reaching into her pocket she took out her mobile phone and rang Laura.

"You okay?" Trish asked.

"Yeah, my parents just asked about twenty-five thousand questions when I got in. But I just told them I was in your place."

"I told Ma the same." Trish giggled.

"So what did you see in there?" Laura asked with a large lump in her throat, she didn't need to explain any further than *in there* for Trish to know exactly where she meant.

"I really don't know. There was four of them in the room and for a moment I could have sworn someone else was standing with them in the shadows, but it all happened so quick."

"They creep me out."

"Yeah, me too!"

Cries of agony stampeded their way up the stairs into her room.

"Sorry, Laura I have to go." She said quickly ending the call.

Chapter 2

"How are my two favourite people in the world doing today?" Daniel asked, walking through the front door after work, interrupting Trish's stroll down memory lane.

"Fine, how was work?" Trish asked, still semi-daydreaming.

"Oh you know, same old same old." He swooped Alan up and hugged him.

Daniel was in his early thirties and was a tall, slim man showing early signs of balding. He spent his days working as an accountant for a small local business.

"He was bold today," Trish said whilst Alan laughed hysterically in his father's arms. "He was trying to go into the Moore's garden."

"Oh, you know kids." Daniel turned to her grinning.

"I don't want him near there. They're weird. One of them was staring at us as we walked by."

"They're just an old couple out of touch with the outside world. Everyone has neighbours like them," Daniel replied, turning back to his son.

"I just don't want him near that place. Okay?"

"Okay." Daniel replied making an over exaggerated sad face to Alan while tickling him. During the giddy raucous Daniel glanced outside.

"Hunny, your friend is outside," he said still enjoying the playful fun with his son.

"What do you mean?" Trish snarled, quickly marching over to the window.

Walking at a snail's pace along the road outside was Frank with his trusted companion, Sam. As the sun glared down on them, she couldn't help but think that they looked like old, dry twigs covered in dirt which were ready to snap at any moment with the slightest force.

Frank looked across the road at her gawping out at him. Trish didn't budge; she just stared back. He then turned away and continued on his slow journey.

He must stink! She thought, watching him pass by her house wearing that large, heavy old coat. For a moment, an image popped into her head of sweat rolling down his old hairy arms, past the sleeve ends of the coat and splashing onto the ground below. She quickly tried to clear her mind.

"Jesus, they're weird." She stepped away from the window.

Daniel looked at her and said, "They're just old and alone."

"I don't care what they are. I just want my son to stay away from that place!"

"Right," Daniel replied with scrunched eye brows.

Of course, the Moore's hadn't always been alone. Frank and Stephanie had a child once. Michael. When Trish was younger, her parent's had often told her about him. The couple had the child later in life, a few years before Trish herself was born. He was your typical newborn who cried un-end for the first number of days after arriving into this world. But the tiny community became a little concerned and uneasy when the days turned into a week of crying. Margret Byrne, who lived right next door to the Moore's, claimed the infant howled in pain through the night and long into the day. It was on a Wednesday afternoon when she finally decided that something was not right and rang the police claiming, "No normal mother would let their child suffer like that."

Within twenty minutes the squad car pulled up outside, the Garda knocked on the door of the already condemned house in the community's eyes. While they waited for a response, a number of people who lived on the road, gathered outside, led by Margret. Every single one of them were ready to hurl abuse and anything they could find at the *terrible* parents inside.

The door opened. The baby cried, and the Garda stepped inside. Of course in the communities eyes, he stepped into some brutal torture dungeon where the child had been submitted to hours of unrelenting torment and pain and the policeman's first response would be to get sick all over his shoes and floor, then immediately call for back up.

A few hate filled, finger pointing minutes passed, the ominous door reopened, and the Garda stepped back outside. He wasn't running, wasn't screaming, or even panicking.

"So what did they do to the poor child?" Margret shouted.

"Nothing," He replied. "The child has intense tummy gas. That's why he is crying so much. His doctor has given him some medication to help it pass and relieve the pain. Listen, give these people some space okay!"

He climbed back into his car, waving towards Stephanie, and drove away.

Margret and the others then turned back to the house where Steph stood cradling the tiny infant in her arms. She didn't express anger, she just looked saddened and hurt at the fact that everyone assumed she was neglecting or harming her beloved child.

Growing up was slightly different for Michael compared to the rest of the kids his age in the local primary school. The main reason being, of course, most of the kids were terrified of his parents, which resulted in him being cast to the side during school hours. Stephanie and Frank would wait at the school gates for the final bell to ring each day and walk their son home no matter hail, rain, or shine. Some of the other parents would glare and sneer at their appearance. Steph with her usual long, platted white hair, gold rings, lucky rabbit's foot, and a long dark skirt which stretched from her tiny waist to her ankles. Frank with his trademark trench coat and crusty warted face. The couple never paid any attention to their audience, just collected their beloved son and went on about their business, not caring that most people thought they weren't fit, too strange, or too weird to be parents.

Michael was an intelligent boy in school. Homework was always in on time, questions in class were always answered, attendance was one hundred percent, and politeness was never in question.

He was a slim boy with dark black hair. Some of the other parents said he was subjected to starvation which was contradicted by his brightness and alertness in school. He always ate lunch by himself. At age seven, he didn't really care if no one sat with him. He was interested in what his mother did from a very young age. Michael would peek in through the keyhole and press his ear against the door when she had participating individuals over to contact their loved ones. However, she always told him that he was too young to get involved in what she practised and she would talk to him about it when the time was right.

As Michael grew older, the bullying in school became worse. The kids in his class would point at him and say things like "Hey, I think I seen your mother fly by the moon last night," or "Doesn't your dad have a house to haunt," "I saw a dead animal on the road today, did your mother do it?"

None would be said in front of Stephanie or Frank when they collected Michael because everyone tried their best not to make eye contact with them or soil their underwear.

The couple spent many long nights consoling their lonesome son as he balled his eyes out.

"Why do they say those things?" He'd cry.

"It's just people being people," Frank would say.

School turned into a mental and physical challenge for Michael. He attempted to block out the insults and laughter and physically took the pushing and shoving. However, Michael wouldn't have to suffer relentless torment past his eleventh birthday.

On the evening Michael died, Steph was in the middle of one of her ceremonies and Frank was struggling to stay awake while watching TV. Michael decided to go out into the crisp night air, which looked like the middle of the day due to the brightness of the full moon. He proceeded to the side of the house where Frank split and stored the firewood. As always, the axe was wedged into the chopping block, which was another popular horror story among the local kids.

"That's where he cuts your head off!" They would say.

Michael had always been warned not to go near it but that night he only wanted to help.

He pressed on, and raised the handle of the axe, its head squeaked in the solid timber. It took a number of hard attempts before the axe finally came loose enough for him to lift. Michael placed logs on the large chopping block from the neat pile Frank kept. The logs cracked as the sharp metal crashed into them. After about five minutes into the work, Michael was fatigued, an axe becomes very heavy after a couple of swings by an eleven-year-old. Under tiring, heavy arms, the axe hopped off the logs, causing him to lose his balance. He regained his composure and then continued. Then he missed the logs altogether and stumbled. An adult might have given up for the night and returned back inside the house, but Michael took one more swing at the log boldly deflecting all of his attacks. Again, Michael stumbled. He missed the log and the entire chopping block.

The swing caused the axe to follow through and smash into the top inside of his right thigh. He instantly dropped the axe and stood there in shock. There was nothing for a moment, then a warm, wet feeling followed by a shooting intense pain. He screamed and shook as the blood pooled on the uneven ground beneath him. Moments later, he collapsed.

Frank was first to see his son bleeding to death at the side of the house. He quickly put pressure on the wound, however the blood continued to spout around his shaking fingers.

"Michael, talk to me!" He said as the young boy's body became colder in his arms.

Screams of a panicked and terrified mother saturated the night air as Stephanie and her participants rushed outside to see what all the commotion was about.

"Quick, call an ambulance," Frank howled.

By the time he finished the sentence there were

two people dialling *999* on their phones.

Stephanie raced across the grass and knelt down on the ground beside her son, which was mostly painted in cooling blood. Her cries and Frank's pleading for any sign of life in his son's body caused a number of neighbours to venture out and up to the Moore's fence.

Ten more minutes passed, the audience peered on in silence as the child lay there still and unresponsive. His parent's desperate pleas for any sign of life were drowned out by fast approaching sirens and blue intermitting lights stabbing their way through the darkness.

By the time the ambulance arrived to the scene, it was already too late. Michael's life had drained from his body into the soil around him.

That had been another dark mark against the Moore's within the community. Neighbours said they were "Bad parents," they "Neglected their son," and "They didn't protect him, which resulted in his death."

The Moore's became even further social recluses, if that was possible at that stage. Frank and Stephanie spent the next number of years mourning their son's death amongst themselves. Fr. Cullen would often offer his services to help the family through the tragic time, but they wanted to manage their feelings of emptiness, hurt, and despair on their own.

Stephanie began doing her readings about a year and a half after Michael's death. Most of her clients were non-locals, mostly due to the haunting, evil reputation which had wrongly befallen the Moore's. The outsiders didn't judge them, and Stephanie liked it that way.

The clock struck 8pm as the rain trickled down the window outside. Stephanie was doing a reading for a young couple who wanted to hear good news about their future. Candlelight filled the room while shadows jumped forward and back along the walls with each flicker. Stephanie first sensed the immense love the couple shared for each other and the bright future they had ahead of them. She then unlocked the *door*, opened it, and scanned the waiting spirits for any sign of trickery or evil, so she could quickly banish them from the entrance. Many dead relatives and friends joined the session to say things like hello, not to worry about them, and that they are happy.

After some time into the session, Stephanie sensed something familiar.

She spotted a glowing outline of a young boy standing in the corner of the room beside a burning candle. She continued her reading for the couple because she often knew that some irrelevant, lonely *guests* would attend the sessions waiting for a chance to speak.

"Some lost souls just wait at the door, waiting for it to open," she would say.

Time passed, and the spirit of the young boy remained in the same position looking at her. The child finally smiled, and she instantly recognised that old, familiar smile and scent floating across in the air. It was Michael.

Her heart radiated with warmth she had not felt in quite some time; a flood of almost uncontrollable emotion flowed through her as those innocent eyes and smile cast themselves across the room. She finished her session without flinching, trying to be as professional as possible to her paying customers, and when she looked towards the corner again, it had darkened slightly. Michael was gone.

It's for the best, she thought. *Now he can finally rest.*

However, that wasn't the last she would see of him. For quite some time after his first appearance, Steph would always recognise a familiar voice and glimmering smile being projected from the corner of the room. Michael would always be standing beside the entrance to the next world, waiting to walk through it and say hello to his mother. Steph would never talk with him because she wanted her boy to be at peace and felt that was the best way to achieve her wish.

She had spoken to him on one occasion; during the second time he appeared to her.

"I'm so sorry for what happened. I think about you every day, and each time my heart breaks a little more. Go and be at peace Michael, I love you so much and always will!"

She never spoke to him after that but always shared a smile every time he connected with her. She was in some way comforted knowing that she could see him from time to time and he could still manage to smile with her after what had happened.

Stephanie confided with Frank about the many times Michael had visited her. Frank was relieved to know that their son was in a way still attached to them and still shared their love, however he wanted Michael to be at peace without coming back over and over again to the place where he died.

Chapter 3

Either while alone or with other people present, "The spirits have no *off* switch," Stephanie often stated, and it wasn't always sunshine, roses, smiles and happy feelings when they came to visit. She learned from a young age that when you willingly open the door to the other side, it also attracts dark spirits to it like a magnet. They're just waiting to get through and fuck with the key holder and anyone else they can get their sadistic, demented, evil hands on. Stephanie would have to use tremendous willpower and abilities to keep the dark ones on the right side of the door! She would have to quickly sieve through them and identify the right candidate to allow into our world.

She knew from a young age that she was a little different than everyone else. She use to hear whispering when she was in a room by herself and see shadows moving in the corner of her eye. She never told anyone because she thought it would pass and didn't think people would believe her.

Her first encounter with an evil spirit occurred when she was only seventeen years old. She lived in Wexford at the time with her parents and brother, Steven. Stephanie had only one best friend who was killed in a crash while travelling home one dark winter's evening. A drunk driver swerved across the road and smacked head on into their tiny car which Mary's father was driving. Mary died at the scene from internal bleeding, her father suffered two broken legs whilst the drunken idiot sat in his car trying to un-blur his vision and figure out what had just happened.

Not long after her burial Mary appeared to Stephanie.

The first night Stephanie was scared shitless. It was the first time a spirit physically—so to speak—appeared in front of her.

"Hey ..." whispered across the dark, swamped room.

"HEY...STEPH." Again the voice floated through the darkness.

The only light was projected from the bright full moon outside the curtains. Steph raised her drowsy self in the old, creaky, wooden bed, wiped her eyes, and looked over across the room. Out of the darkness stepped Mary, wearing a beautiful white dress which clung to her slender body. Her black hair flowed with *life*, and she smiled saying, "Hello."

Stephanie gasped almost every bit of air in the room into her lungs. She became slightly dizzy while gripping the multi-patterned, heavy blanket as tightly as she could.

"Am I dreaming?" she said through her gasps.

"No, it's me." Mary grinned.

"How ... am I?" Stephanie struggled through her thoughts to find the words, "seeing you ...?"

"It's your gift," Mary replied.

"I don't understand."

"You will in time."

Over the next number of nights, at the same time, Mary would appear in Stephanie's bedroom. The pair would talk for some time before Mary would say she had to go. Stephanie was bewildered by her new found ability.

The following Thursday night, right on time, Mary stepped out of the darkness and into the room, but there was something slightly different about her. At first, Steph noticed she seemed emotionless, older, and slightly taller. When Mary spoke, it was with a deeper voice, and her eyes contained darkness and a glare that made Stephanie feel uncomfortable and vulnerable.

"Why don't you join me?" Mary whispered in a low, forceful tone.

"What do you mean?"

"I was your only friend, and now we are both alone. Come and join me. I'll help you cross over." She grinned.

Stephanie shivered in her bed as a halo of black shadows pulsated around her so called dead friend's spirit.

"You're not Mary are you?" she asked as the cold sweat slowly trickled down her back, the air around her turned cold.

The spirit grinned and tilted its head slightly, not responding.

"Are you?" Stephanie asked again.

Mary laughed an evil, sporadic, high pitch tone.

"You stupid fucking bitch!" The entity snarled at her. "Did you really think you can contact my world and find only good? Set me free. I'll show you how pathetic that word is!"

Every muscle in Stephanie's body stiffened.

"Here, I'll show you," The spirit said.

The entity slowly approached the bed. At first, it began snapping teeth out of its mouth by hand, tossing them across the floor like old, unwanted one cent coins. With every forceful jerk came a horrendous tear as each tooth was ripped from the gum.

"This isn't happening," Stephanie frantically told herself.

"Oh it is," whispered through her mind.

The entity then tore a hole in the white dress it was wore, whilst blood trickled from its evil mouth.

"How about a souvenir from your friend?" asked the spirit whose only motive for stepping through the spiritual door was to torture the first living person it came across.

The spirit placed both index fingers into *Mary's* belly button and ripped it open. The skin pulled apart like wet paper as the contents of her stomach spilled out and splashed onto the floor; the spirit shoved both hands inside, tore at some internal organs, and then held its bloodied hands out to Stephanie,

"Here have some!" The spirit laughed.

Every single ounce of Stephanie's will wanted to scream for help, but she knew that wouldn't help. Instead, the teenager closed her eyes and told herself, "I don't want this to happen, and I have the key to lock the door again."

Stephanie concentrated, squeezing her eyes tight enough the lids almost overlapped each other while she began repeating in her head, "I opened the door, and I want you to leave! No one asked YOU to come here!"

Loud ringing filled her ears. Salty sweat rolled down her face. Pressure formed in her skull, throbbing and pounding through the building strain, however she remained focused on banishing the unwanted evil. Then, just as soon as the pain appeared, it was gone. The room was empty. The teeth had disappeared. She was alone once more.

Knocking rapped on her bedroom door half a breath before her parents rushed into the room.

"Are you okay? We heard you talking to someone," her mother asked racing over to the bed.

"I'm fine, Mam. Don't worry about it. I was just dreaming!"

After some general chit chat and checking her forehead, Stephanie's parents returned to the comfort of their bed.

Following that night, Stephanie was careful opening the door to the other side. She had experienced the trickery and the power of an evil she didn't want to witness again.

It was nice to wish.

Chapter 4

Trish and Daniel were busy celebrating Alan's tenth birthday at home on a fine, glowing June summer's day. The soundtrack of children's laughter and their parents' occasional, "Calm down please," echoed around the house. The party started at 2pm, and most of the guests arrived soon afterwards. The alluring smoke from the barbeque weaved its way through the crowd as they enjoyed the always welcome hot weather.

"Those sausages look lovely. Are they nearly done?" Declan asked, looking at the long lumps of meat hissing and sizzling in the flames.

Declan lived two doors up from Trish and Daniel and never missed an occasion where free food was available. He was a short, overweight man who always wore shirts or jumpers which clung to his big frame for dear life. He lived with his wife and two sons and worked as a truck driver for a local delivery company in Arklow.

"Almost ready," replied Daniel, turning them amongst the weaving flames.

Trish made her way around the garden, making sure that everyone had enough to drink and eat. They had a long table made up of smaller plastic tables put side by side covered with a table cloth. It was decorated with big bowls of peanuts, sweets, crisps, various different types of drinks, and party poppers and hats for the children. Underneath the table, in the shade, was a huge ice bucket containing various bottles and cans of beer for the adults.

Moments later, Daniel placed a cooked sausage into a bread roll and handed it to Declan, who was drooling. He devoured it in seconds. Daniel then walked over and took another beer from the bucket. The ice cold water ran along his hand as he opened the can and then took a sip.

"It's a fantastic day for it," Trish said joining him.

"It is hunny. The kids are having a great time." He took another drink, watching the children giggling and chasing each other around the garden.

"I'll bring out the cake soon." Trish smiled.

"No problem. I'll keep the hot food coming," Daniel said kissing her on the cheek, returning to the barbeque with his cold beverage.

Cheers and laughter filled the air the moment Trish stepped out from the kitchen into the back yard carrying a sponge cake covered in white frosting with *Happy Birthday Alan* scribed across the top of it. The final decoration was ten burning candles around its edges. Trish carefully tried to prevent the candles from blowing out as she set the cake on the table.

"Where's my birthday boy?" she shouted as a crowd of adults and giddy children gathered around her.

"Found him," Daniel said a brief moment later,

stepping towards her holding the young boy's hand who grinned from ear to ear. Alan wore a navy jacket with a large *Happy 10th Birthday* badge attached to it.

Everyone began to sing *Happy Birthday*, followed by applause.

He joined his mother's side, and she whispered, "Don't forget to make a wish."

He leaned towards the cake, took a deep breath, and blew out all the candles in one full blow as the crowd cheered him on. Trish removed the smouldering candles from the cake while Daniel stepped back to admire the scene. Emotions of happiness and fulfilment washed over Daniel watching his son getting ready to cut his cake. Trish allowed Alan to hold the knife while cupping his hand within hers.

Hails of hoorays echoed after the first cut was made, then Trish began to dish up, giving Alan the first slice.

I knew he'd be the first one. Daniel grinned to himself, looking at Declan standing in line with the kids.

Where does he fit it all? He wondered.

"Terrific party, Daniel. The kids love it," Owen, Daniel's best friend, said.

Owen was a tall, slim man whose hair showed signs of premature greying. He worked for a local carpenter and lived with his wife and daughter.

"Thanks, man. Glad you and Amy could make it."

"We wouldn't have missed it for the world," Owen said, taking a bottle of beer from the ice bucket. "You got the weather for it as well."

"Yeah, thank God. At least it's a change from all the rain we've been getting." Daniel smiled.

"Is it okay if we go play out on the road?" Alan asked Trish.

"Okay, but stay on our road. I'll be watching," she said, words firm.

"Okay. Thanks, Mammy," Alan said, picking up a football then going onto the road with Stephen and Anthony, Declan and Bridgett's sons; David, another local boy; and Christina, Owen's daughter.

"Careful now, kids!" Amy shouted after them, then turned back and continuing talking with the other Moms.

Once out on the road, the kids started playing *piggy in the middle*. Alan was on one side of the group and Stephen was on the opposite while the others stood between them jumping as high as they could to catch the ball every time it was hurled up and down the road above them. They laughed and shouted with joy with every failed attempt to grab the ball.

"It's your turn in the middle now," David said after catching the ball thrown by Stephen.

"Not for long," Stephen said, giving him a friendly nudge.

The children continued playing their game. Moments later, David noticed that Stephen was very close to catching the ball when he was throwing it to

Alan, so he tossed it as hard as he could through the pleasant country air. Looking up, the bright blue ball momentarily blended into the sky above as it over shot Alan's waiting grasp. The kids giddily ran up the road after the straying ball, all hoping to be the first to reach it. Just as Alan was about to pick it up, from the corner of his eye, he saw a right foot firmly connect with it. The ball flew up the road, bounced over an old swaying fence, and ploughed into the Moore's intimidating front garden. Alan darted straight as the nerves began to bubble inside him. He turned and looked at Stephen who stared at the ball coming to a halt half way up the lawn.

"I'm not getting it," he quickly mumbled.

"You kicked it!" Alan replied.

"So, it's your football!"

The scared response did nothing to sway Alan.

As the two boys stared at one another, the group slowly walked up the road towards the house of their nightmares. Hundreds of ghost stories had manifested themselves from that place over the years. Alan placed a hand delicately onto the dry, rotting fence, he turned, music danced its way up the road from his parent's house. He didn't want to go into the dreaded yard, but he didn't want to leave the ball there either, because he had only got it as a gift that very day.

"Keep a look out, okay?" he said, building up courage and climbing through a broken piece of the fencing; the others stared on holding their breath.

Alan slowly moved along the grass trying to keep one eye on the ball and another on that horrendous front door splotched with very old, crusty brown paint. Every part of him wanted to turn and run, but he was so close to the ball. The closer he got, the more his nerves grew.

They eat children. They'll eat me! Echoed in his mind.

The children standing at the fence could barely watch.

Alan was in reaching distance of the ball when the old, wooden front door slowly creaked open. Alan, who had planned on running, froze. All the other kids ducked as low as they possibly could. Stephanie stepped out into the sunlight and immediately shielded her eyes with her left, veiny hand. Her thin, hunched over body was clothed in an old, long black dress with worn black shoes. She smiled at Alan holding her lucky rabbit's foot and began walking towards him. The child was terrified and he began to cry uncontrollably.

"We should run," Anthony whispered.

"She'll see us," Stephen said.

As Stephanie slowly reached Alan, he wet himself. She stretched out her arm. He gasped with terror. She leaned passed him, and picked up the ball.

"Here you go child. Don't cry." She smiled, holding the ball out to him.

"Alan, come here now!" Trish shouted from the roadside.

Alan quickly turned and ran to his mother,

leaving Steph holding the ball.

"What have I told you about that place?" Taking his hand, Trish turned towards the other children. "Come on everyone."

Walking home with the kids, she glanced over her shoulder at Stephanie who was still standing there looking towards her, holding Alan's football.

"Go play in the garden now, okay." She told the children, opening the front door and wiping the tears from her son's tormented face.

"Don't ever go in there again, Alan. Do you hear me?"

The boy nodded.

"Good boy. Now go get a shower, change, and go play with your friends." She smiled, to reassure him he was safe.

Alan went upstairs to the bathroom while Trish returned to the party.

"Is everything alright?" Daniel asked, grabbing another beer from the ice bucket.

"I went to check on them, and Alan was in the Moore's yard."

"Is he okay?"

"He's fine. Just got a little upset; they give me the fucking creeps," she said, making an overly elaborated shivering gesture.

"I know, love. Let's enjoy the rest of the day," Daniel said, giving her a hug.

Ten minutes later, Alan re-joined his friends in the garden. They played well into the evening while

35

the adults drank beer, ate, and talked. On the horizon, the sun resembled a drowning person struggling with all their might to keep their head above the water, as it cast its final light across the sky. Many of the guests and children had left the party as darkness saturated the countryside. Owen, Amy, and Christina were the only party goers that remained.

"Here, let me give you a hand cleaning up," Amy said to Trish.

"Don't worry about it. I'll clean it in the morning." She smiled.

"Well, I guess we better be going. Thanks for a wonderful day guys," Owen said, collecting his jacket.

"No problem at all," Daniel said, walking with them to the door.

Daniel then returned outside and sent Alan to the bathroom to brush his teeth before going to bed. He sat with Trish by the glowing outdoor heater which radiated moderate heat and a mild smell of gas. The garden looked like a storm had burst through it, tossing paper cups and plates all over the place; used party poppers and their multi-coloured stringy contents decorated the table and surrounding grass like a torn, tattered blanket. A slight breeze kissed their cheeks.

"It still gets chilly enough when the sun goes down, doesn't it." Daniel said cupping Trish's left hand in his right.

"Yeah, it was a great day though. Everyone really enjoyed themselves."

"Alan looked like he had fun. I'll get up early in the morning and help you clean up the place," he said.

"No problem. Listen, about Alan, he wet himself earlier when he was in the Moore's garden getting his ball. I didn't want to tell you to ruin your day."

"Wet himself ... Did they do anything to him?" Daniel asked almost leaping to his feet.

"No, he was just scared, and so was I, to be honest. I just hate that place."

"I know. They're just old people set in their ways." He settled back into the seat.

"It's not that. I've seen and heard some weird things at that house over the years. Something just isn't right about them," she replied.

Chapter 5

Trish recalled the night when Rachel and Laura snuck over to the Moore's house with her; she recalled the smile Stephanie gave her through the window as something else moved in the corner of the room before she quickly ducked below the window. She recalled ringing Laura later that night and having to quickly end the call because of her mother's cries filling the house. That was the night her father died.

Trish quickly threw her phone onto the fluffy bed duvet and raced downstairs to her mother who was hunched over in the kitchen sobbing her heart out.

"What's wrong?" Trish asked while her mother's tears continued to splash against the tiled floor.

"What's wrong Mum?" taking her in her arms.

"It's your father ... he's ... he's in the hospital." Her words somehow made its way through all the shallow breathing and crying.

A wave of fear, uncertainty, and panic crashed over Trish. "What happened?"

"I don't know. It was the guards who called ... he's ... he's dead Patricia." She stuttered, before erupting into a fit of loud cries and despair.

At that moment, time stopped. Pain engulfed every part of Trish. Not the kind of pain you feel when you scald yourself with boiling water or sizzling cooking oil. The emotional pain that's a combination of emptiness, sadness, hurt, and also the torment of not knowing what had just happened to her father. She too spontaneously broke down while cradling her mother in her arms.

"We have to go to the hospital. That's where they brought him," her mother finally whimpered.

"Okay," Trish said swaying uncontrollably to her feet as the shock sank farther into her body. "I'll ring a taxi."

"No need. The guards said they'll bring us. They will be here in ten minutes."

The sweet smell of Bridgett's homemade cooking still lingered in the room. Various kitchen utensils still had the remains of the scone ingredients on them. She hadn't had time to clean them before her world was unexpectedly turned upside down, inside out and dropkicked straight out from underneath her.

Bridgett changed out of her slippers into some flat black shoes she always wore, which she had planned on throwing in the bin because they always pinched the sides of her feet but never got around to it. Which was the least of her worries now. Meanwhile, Trish used the bathroom.

"They've got it wrong. Dad is fine," she said, trying to convince herself, while drying her hands and looking at her morbid reflection in the small, square, bathroom mirror. Trish then joined her mother in the sitting room and waited for the Gardaí to arrive.

Two young Gardaí collected Bridgett and Trish; the women didn't recognise them, probably due to the constant rotation of newly trained personnel at the local Garda station.

"Tell me what happened?" Bridgett pleaded on the way to the hospital.

"A passer-by found him lying face down in the middle of the road. She called an ambulance, and he was declared dead at the scene. The ambulance service then contacted us and we took a statement from the individual. Your husband was taken to the hospital for a post-mortem. I think the doctors should explain the rest," the driver replied as delicately as he could.

Both mother and daughter couldn't accept what they heard. Trish couldn't help but feel like a common criminal sitting in the back on the Garda car.

How many scumbags have sat in this seat? She thought.

To make things worse, there was no cage or glass separation between the back seats and front seats like in the movies.

So what's to stop a degenerate from attacking the driver while they are being hauled away?

Trish's mind quickly snapped back to thoughts of her dead father's body lying on a cold, stainless steel tray in the morgue being poked and prodded at like some worthless piece of roadkill.

As they drove through Arklow, Trish watched

people walking up and down the street, talking and laughing together.

I wish I was one of those people right now but, instead, I've just lost my Dad and my life will never be the same again, she thought, exhaling loudly.

The police parked the car at the A&E department located on the right hand side of the large building. A gentle drizzle began to float to the ground as the officers escorted the women inside. The A&E department was a large room with twenty bed cubicles, most of them occupied by injured or ill people, separated by thin, green plastic curtains. When the Gardaí stepped into the room, a young nurse approached them wearing a standard uniform—a white nurse's top with black bottoms— she was small and thin with acne splattered across her face.

"We are here in relation to Peter Quinn," one of the Gardaí said.

"Just one moment please," she said turning from them.

She disappeared down the corridor located on the other side of the A&E department and returned moments later with a greying, middle-aged man dressed in black slacks, a white shirt with a blue tie, and a stethoscope draped around his neck.

"Dr. Fitzgerald." He introduced himself shaking Bridgett's hand. "I'm sorry for your loss."

Funny how those words mean fuck all when they are being said to someone in the situation, Trish thought.

"Can I see my husband?" A broken Bridgett asked.

"Certainly. Follow me," he responded.

The doctor led the individuals from A&E down a long white corridor furnished with hospital beds, carts, nursing stations, and some scattered recovering patients decorated up and down it, trying to break the monotony of the slow passing hours. They turned right, and the doctor took a small key card from his pocket then swiped it across a pad on the wall. The two large stainless steel doors opened automatically.

"The mortuary is just down here." He directed with his left palm.

They continued down the hallway, which was completely free from obstructions, and reached two more large stainless steel doors. Again, the doctor swiped his key card. The doors opened, and they stepped into a room completely covered in stainless steel. On one side of the room, there were a number of trolleys placed neatly together in front of a number of locker doors.

That must be where they store the dead bodies. Cascaded through Trish's mind.

Cubicles, almost identical to the ones in the A&E department, took up the opposite of the room. Bridgett instantly noticed one of the curtains was closed.

"He is just here," the doctor said, approaching the curtain.

Both Garda's remained near the entrance to the

morgue to allow the Quinn's some space to take in the visual shock. Dr. Fitzgerald pulled back the curtain to reveal a slender pale frame, clothed in a chequered blue and white hospital gown, lying on a cold trolley. A couple of day's stubble growth stood from his dead skin like the tips of shiny silver needles. The women began sobbing, looking at their loved one's lifeless body lying in front of them. Dr. Fitzgerald stood aside.

"What happened?" Bridgett spluttered holding her cold, dead husband's hand in hers, bringing the reality of it all crashing home.

"Tests show he suffered a cardiac arrest Mrs. Quinn."

"Daddy wake up. Please, wake up!" Trish screamed.

His face remained solid as stone. No light returned to the dark pitted holes hiding his eyes. He did not reply. He was gone, and no amount of words could help ease the pain both wife and daughter experienced.

"I'm sorry for your loss," Dr. Fitzgerald said once more whilst Bridgett and Trish held onto each other to prevent one another falling to the floor.

"Why don't we go to my office?" he asked, pulling the curtain in front of Peter's lifeless body once more.

The hospital released Peter's body the next day, and he was buried the following Tuesday.

The Quinn family were extremely thankful to

their local community for the support they received during their bereavement. Neighbours came by to cook meals, collect groceries, and assist with household chores—anything to help relieve the stress from the family. Quite a large amount of flowers and Mass cards were sent to their house the week following Peter's funeral. The only Mass card which made Trish uncomfortable was the one they received on the day of Peter's burial.

Bridgett and Trish had returned home that evening. When Bridgett opened the door, a single white envelope sat alone in the hall. She picked it up and opened it.

"I suppose they want to express their condolences too," she said, handing it to Trish.

The teenager glanced at the card signed by Francis and Stephanie Moore. A chill ran through her. She didn't have the mental capacity to think about their sick motives and deal with her father's untimely death at the same time.

They say that time is a great healer, but for Trish, every day that passed was worse than the last. Days multiplied the time to give countless hours of unending pain without her father.

A month passed and Trish still felt the exact same she did when she first heard the news; afraid, uncertain, and lost. She took part as best she could in her mundane routine of breakfast, school, homework, bed, and at the weekends, hanging out with her friends in an attempt to keep her sanity.

Bridgett did her best to maintain a normal household as much as possible for the sake of her daughter. She had breakfast ready in the mornings when Trish got up and dinner ready in the evenings when she came home. She would help Trish with her homework and give her space when she needed it.

It was a beautiful sunny day in mid-April. The sky was blue, the air was warm, birds were singing, and Peter had been under the soil for almost six weeks. Trish made her usual journey home from school in Arklow which took her approximately thirty minutes on foot. The road was quite busy.

Ignorant assholes! she thought to herself, carrying her school jacket under her arm whilst every purring engine passed closely beyond her, some almost clipping her.

She reached her road, turned left, and noticed Stephanie tending to something in what resembled a front garden. It was dominated by weeds more than grass. Stephanie turned and spotted the teenager, she smiled and began walking towards the fence; she was a little quicker on her feet back then. She wore a tattered, long grey skirt with a white t-shirt, however her small, slender frame was still evident beneath.

"I'm sorry for your loss, child," she said leaning on the fence while Trish nervously stepped closer to her.

This is all I need. She already didn't like the couple, and she certainly didn't want to engage in any form of conversation with them. Trish stared at the ground beneath her as she walked passed Steph.

"I understand what you're going through, child. I can help you say good bye properly if you want?"

Steph stared for a moment at the teenager stepping farther away from her, and she resigned to picking some weeds from around the drooping, weary, sun-starved daffodils at her feet.

Reaching home, Trish sat with her mother and ate some dinner made up of potatoes, sweet cabbage, and salty bacon splashed with some gravy. Trish's favourite dinner. She loved it when she was younger and her appetite for it hadn't worn off yet.

"Here comes the aeroplane" followed by an attempt at an engine noise was Peter's preferred approach to feeding his daughter when she was younger, but she needed little encouragement to open her mouth when bacon and cabbage was on the menu.

After Trish savoured her last mouthful of bacon and mash, she placed the plate into the sink along with her glass which still had a ring of milk stained around its brim. Bridgett always liked doing the washing up, and she especially favoured doing it after her loss because she could daydream out through the window to help get her mind off things.

Meanwhile, Trish went to her bedroom with the intention to begin doing her homework, but she couldn't get the encounter with Stephanie out of her head. She lay on the inviting, soft, comfortable mattress.

I can help you say goodbye? She pondered. She didn't need to think much more about the sentence because she was almost certain about what the weirdo up the road meant.

Loneliness weighed heavily on Trish as every heart ripping second without her father slowly ticked away. Sure, she had Bridgett who did the best she could for her daughter, but Trish missed her father's smile, his positive outlook on life, and his famous saying: "Anything can be done with good old sweat and hard work." She missed his quirky sense of humour, and most of all, she missed talking to him.

She couldn't help but imagine what would it be like if she could talk to him once more. *What would I say? I miss you? What's being dead really like? Is there a white light at the end of the tunnel? Does heaven exist? Are you at peace? What would anyone ask if they had the opportunity to really speak to someone on the other side?*

Maybe scary Steph can help me?

Trish couldn't believe the thought crept into her mind. But the more she thought about it, the more it seemed to make sense. She can talk to the dead, and the girl wanted to say goodbye to her father in person, so to speak.

A few days passed, and every evening Trish walked home, Steph was nowhere in sight. There was no way the teenager was going to approach that house again uninvited after her last experience, she'd be chopped to pieces for sure.

How do I even start a conversation with her if I do see

her?

She contemplated on an overcast Thursday afternoon, returning home from school. Rounding the corner towards home, and Stephanie was walking towards the ajar front door to her dreaded house. Images of Peter smiling and echoes of his voice ran through Trish's head whilst the adrenaline surging through her made her shake.

It's now or never! A loud voice roared between her ears.

"Excuse me," stuttered passed her lips.

Stephanie didn't hear it.

Trish swallowed a small amount of saliva to help moisten her dry throat and stepped a little closer to the Moore's house.

"Sorry ... excuse me ..." she said once again.

This time her soft nervous words where heard. Stephanie turned towards Trish and smiled.

"Yes, child?"

"What did you mean when you said you can help me say goodbye?"

Stephanie leaned down and placed some old, worn, green-stained gardening gloves on the front door step then shuffled to the edgy teenager.

Run ... scream for help ... defend yourself ... close your eyes! Those thoughts juggled around the young girl's mind, but she held her ground. She clinched her jaw and gripped the strap of the school bag tossed over her shoulder tighter and tighter with every approaching step Steph gained on her. Every tense muscle in her legs wanted to release and run as fast they could, but she had to do this.

"I have a rare gift, my dear, which I can use to help you speak with your dad if you would like to," the old woman explained.

Trish felt different, hearing words coming from the horse's mouth rather than word of mouth around the locality, Steph really sounded fucking crazy. Steph sensed the girl's uneasiness.

"Listen, child, each one of us has a gift. Some of us are fantastic musicians, some of us are great painters, writers, builders, singers, and so on. My gift is a little different than them, but it is a gift nonetheless, and I use it to help individuals like you if they want me to."

Trish couldn't speak. She had spent years hearing all the stories and shitting herself every time she seen or even heard the Moore's being mentioned but here she was talking with the witch she had feared for so long.

"I don't know ..." Trish finally managed to say.

"It's completely up to you my dear. Feel free to call on me when you wish."

Steph turned, not wanting to put any pressure of the girl, and walked away.

"Wait ..." she called after her. "I want to say goodbye to my father properly. I never had the chance to..."

Trish's eyes began to swell with moisture. "I just want to talk to him."

"I understand. Why don't you come over around eight this evening?" Stephanie said, smiling.

Alarms bells rang in Trish's head; there was no way she was going into that house at night.

"Is it okay if I come back in about an hour? I just want to grab something to eat first."

"Absolutely no problem, dear. Just knock on the door and I'll let you in."

Stephanie smiled once more and returned to her house. Trish couldn't quite tell if it was one of sincerity or one hiding a sinister motive.

Dinner was gobbled frantically as the teenager wondered if she was doing the right thing.

What if they trap me? What if I'm never seen again? Tormented her mind.

There was no way she could talk to her mother about this because the response would be, "What the hell are you thinking?"

After finishing her dinner, Trish then quickly went to her room and put on some fresh clothes.

"I'll be home soon, okay, Mam?" she said, closing the front door behind her.

"Not too late, okay!" Bridgett shouted after her.

Trish anxiously clenched her jaw so tight she thought she might snap some teeth during the walk to the Moore's house. Shivers ran across her spine, not from the cold, but from the thought of finally stepping foot inside the house that had haunted her thoughts—and sometimes her dreams—for so long.

She reached the gate leading to the decrepit house; she looked towards the front door, which was already opening, Steph then stepped out from the dark interior and greeted the teenager.

Chapter 6

"Come on, hunny. Let's go in out of the cold," Daniel said as he stood up and reached across to turn off the outdoor heater as the night shadows continued to further darken the evening. Trish had nodded off in his arms; and she strained to open her eyes fully.

"I'm not looking forward to getting up to this messy garden in the morning." She smiled.

"Me neither." Daniel laughed. "But at least everyone enjoyed the party, eh?"

Trish smiled, nodding in agreement.

The pair went into the house, which was thankfully warmer than outside. Trish went upstairs to get ready for bed while Daniel made his usual rounds downstairs, checking that all the windows were locked—or locked slightly open, depending on the weather—and also checked that both the front and back door where secured by pressing firmly down on their handles once or twice to ensure that they wouldn't open. When he was satisfied, he joined Trish in the bedroom, who was in her nightwear within the large wooden framed bed.

The bedroom itself was always kept tidy by Trish; she often had a few harsh words for Daniel if he didn't pick up his clothes the next morning after himself. It had a large wooden wardrobe alongside the bed which overflowed with women's clothes and a tiny space reserved on the right hand side for Daniel to squeeze his items onto a mixture of wooden and strained wire hangers. A strong oak dressing table with an adjustable mirror stood beside the wardrobe, housing mostly a complex collection of woman's deodorants, makeup and perfumes. The room was decorated with cream wallpaper splattered with red roses all over it and a wooden floor which Daniel had often cursed in the cold winter mornings when he had to tip toe across it barefoot to grab fresh socks.

"I'm looking forward to getting some sleep tonight." Daniel yawned while getting undressed. He then quickly stepped across the cool wood, switched off the light, and then climbed into the comfort of the warm bed. Within minutes, he was snoring as Trish lay there listening to her husband's terrible noise.

Lying there, staring at the dark ceiling, random thoughts ran through her mind. Then an old memory, which was still as clear as day to her, projected itself.

She was a teenager again, walking towards the Moore's house. She remembered how cold the sweat felt between every finger, and the chills that ran through her entire body. She remembered the smile Stephanie threw at her as she greeted her at the crumbling old door step.

"Come on in, dear." She grinned. Trish nervously stepped through the door, and the intoxicating smell of burning coal and firewood cracked against her face. The room was dark and decorated with layers of mould surrounding the clammy window. Frank sat by the fire, with a shaggy dog sitting on his lap and greeted her with a smile and nod.

"This way darling," Stephanie said, guiding her towards the room adjacent to the sitting room.

Stepping through the creaking door, Trish was met by the smell of incense, as the candlelight swayed its way throughout the ominous room. She noticed the old table sitting in the middle of the room with equally outdated chairs standing at either side.

"Go ahead, child. Sit down. There is nothing to be afraid of," Stephanie said, encouraging the girl, while removing her old multi-coloured shawl and placing it onto a wooden coat stand.

Trish approached the chair and nervously lowered herself into place. Every inch of her body quivered as the woman of her nightmares placed herself across from her. *Why the hell am I doing this? I should leave while I still can.*

"There is no need to be so scared, my dear. Everything will be okay. I'm going to help you."

The words didn't help much, but the fond thoughts of the girl's beloved father drove her to remain calm. *What if this actually works?* She thought while fear and intrigue wormed its way around the young girl's mind. Meanwhile Steph reached across, struck a match, and lit the lonesome candle on the table.

"I know you're scared, but there really is no need to be, okay? I know how people feel about me, but I hope I can change your opinion."

Trish witnessed a slight sadness in this undoubtedly pure evil woman's eyes, and for the first time, she couldn't help but feel a little sorry for her. *What if everyone was wrong about them? What if the people in the community were the real monsters? Tormenting this couple for no reason besides their own selfish, narrow-minded opinions.*

"When did you realise you could do this?" the girl asked, settling into the atmosphere.

Smiling, Stephanie replied, "I knew I was different from a very young age, but I learned to deal with it. Most people think I'm—we're—crazy, but it's really not all that unusual, is it? Some people may be like me and not realise it. Also, spirits have a number of ways to let the most sceptical individuals know they are not alone, even if they don't know it at the time. For example: have you ever been in bed late at night, and are just about to drift off to sleep when you suddenly jump or twitch for absolutely no reason? That's them, my girl. They're in the room with you. Letting you know they are there."

Actually, that has happened to me, Trish thought, wide eyed and mouth open.

"But don't worry," Steph continued. "You have to possess a gift like mine to open the door, or unquestionably will them into your life before they can enter this world. Are you ready to begin?" Stephanie asked, reaching underneath her chair.

Trish nodded.

From beneath the chair Stephanie pulled a large,

thick, brown leather belt which was attached to a short old heavy duty chain bolted securely to the floor. Trish's face collapsed with shock, as the elderly woman forced the belt around her tiny waist. Fastening it into position, she took a padlock out of her pocket and clamped it in place. She then reached across the table and instructed the bewildered girl in front of her to take the key.

"This is just a precaution my dear, just in case the wrong one gets through," Stephanie said, leaning back in her chair.

The words didn't help reduce the visual unease in front of her. *Am I meant to feel better or worse now?* The young girl wondered. *Was she wearing that contraption when we snuck up to the house that evening? Why is she wearing it?*

"Shall we begin?" The woman's voice interrupted Trish's churning thoughts. "I'm going to try contacting your father and let him speak through me."

"Okay," Trish replied. She couldn't back out now. Her only wish was to speak with her father again.

"Just remember, don't give me back that key until you know for sure it's me."

The girl had little time to question how she would know if it *was* her. As Stephanie began to mumble some words, Trish wondered what the hell she had got herself into. Glancing around the room, the candles began to flicker and a number of them on the old shelving went out altogether. The room grew darker as an unsettling atmosphere grew around the table. Trish's eyes fell back to the old woman in front of her. She was motionless, with hands firmly resting on the armrests and head facing the ground.

"Are you okay?" she muttered.

No reply.

"Hey, are you alright?" she asked a little louder, reaching across the table to try and shove Stephanie back to life.

Just before touching her hand, Stephanie violently swung back in the chair. Head facing the ceiling, she took a loud deep inhale as her back arched in the seat. The woman then contorted viciously in the seat. So much so, Trish thought she was going to hear bones snapping at any moment. Steph repeatedly jumped in the seat as weird, deep, raspy sounds and gasps echoed from her distorted mouth. Grinding her teeth loudly, she stared blankly at the ceiling as the wild convulsions continued. Finally, she slowed and lowered her head once more. Saliva drooled from Steph's mouth. Trish sat in disbelief.

Without warning, Stephanie sat rigid in the chair, staring expressionless at the girl in front of her. Her face was pale and her pupils were dilated. Slowly, she raised her hand and wiped the excessive drool from the left side of her mouth with the back of her hand.

"Dad?" the girl whispered.

Stephanie cracked an unnerving smile across the table.

"Is that you?" the girl continued.

Stephanie laughed hysterically.

"I'm not your fucking father, you stupid little bitch. Now, give me the fucking key!" she demanded, holding her hand out, waiting for the horrified girl to cooperate.

Fear encased the young girl as her body became tense in the seat.

"Give me the fucking key now!" the *woman* demanded in a deep voice, aggressively standing to her feet, clawing at the padlock, and falling into the seat again due to her short restraint.

"Who are you?" Trish whispered breathlessly.

A slow evil laugh crept its way around the ever darkening room.

"Set me free, and I'll show you!" the woman replied slamming her fist hard, rattling the table. Her other hand gripped the armrest of the chair tightly, causing her fingernails to buckle under the pressure.

"No."

It was clear now that it wasn't her father in front of her, but an evil force that possessed the woman.

"This whore won't keep me locked in here forever. I'll get out, and I promise I'll see you again soon, Patricia!"

A cold tremor ran through Trish's body and she almost wet herself upon hearing the unearthly being uttering her name.

"How do you know my name?" asked the girl.

A sinister grin etched its way across her face, and

with that, Stephanie released a loud sigh. Some colour returned to her face as she rubbed her tired, throbbing head.

"Was it him?" she asked.

"Who? My Dad?" the confused girl asked, who just wanted to get the hell out of there. The dread she had for that house and its residents before had multiplied one hundred times over.

"No, not your father. He calls himself Natas, and he is getting stronger," Stephanie quickly replied. "Tell me, dear, do you believe in life after death?"

The woman examined the bruising growing on her hand, clearly the table had won the battle.

"I suppose so." The girl whimpered.

"Well, many may not like to hear this, but there are evil spirits and demons on the other side also, and Natas seems to be one of the stronger ones. A torturous beast. He has been with me before and it is getting harder and harder to banish him. I hope I haven't scared you too much, I can try again to reach your father in a moment."

"No." Trish quickly replied, throwing the key across the table and running from the house, promising herself never to go back there again. She didn't care about the rationality involved with her experience, all she felt was Stephanie tricked her, became aggressive towards her, and had just proven that all the stories about that place were true. She was lucky to be alive.

Chapter 7

Alan had turned sixteen, and like every other teenager, didn't have one care in the world. A common school day for him included copying some homework from the night before from a friend, struggling to stay awake in class, and getting out of the building as quickly as possible once the final bell rang. Like Trish so many years ago, he walked to and from his education. He often glanced into the Moore's dank property and wondered how someone could live in such a miserable place. He was thankful he was at an age where he was sharp enough to stay away from the haunted shithole, so much so he always walked on the opposite side of the road if he wasn't accompanied by his friends Stephen and Anthony. Of course, his friends made fun of him, saying that he was chicken shit. He would always laugh it off saying "not a chicken, just smart."

Every *haunted* house, no doubt, has been the centre of a truth or dare game among teenagers, and the Moore's house was no different.

It was a windy, gloomy Friday afternoon, and the three boys made their home early from school. The cold drizzle pressed against their faces as they rounded the corner towards the decrepit Moore's residence. Aided by the gusts, some of the roof tiles waved at them as they stepped closer to the house of many horrors. Each window was darker than the one that barely stood beside it and the once drooping wooden fence had now completely surrendered to the elements and in places fell to the damp ground beneath it.

"How many people do you think have died in that house?" Anthony asked, grinning at Alan.

"One, at least!" Alan shot back, thinking of Michael whom had drew his final breath beside the mouldy concrete wall.

"Do you think they still have the body in there?" Stephen continued smiling at his brother and then nudged Alan, causing him to resettle the school bag on his right shoulder.

"I bet they are looking out at us right now."

Those words forced Alan to glance towards the ragged old curtains, as they bulged in front of the darkness behind them.

"I dare you to go in," Anthony said, nodding towards the building.

Alan paused for a moment as the wind grew around them.

"Leave him alone, he's scared." Stephen laughed.

"Fuck off, you." was the quick reply.

"Well, go on then. Prove it. Go and find out how many bodies they have hidden inside. We'll stand and keep an eye out."

This must be everyone's worst nightmare; being asked to do something you're sacred shitless to do and the very people who will judge you on your reaction are looking on to see how you respond. Tormented Alan's mind.

"They're in there. How the hell do you think I'm going to do this?" Alan said, trying to escape from the unnerving situation he found himself in.

"No, they aren't. The lights are off. Knock on the door first and, even if they answer, you can outrun them," Anthony returned.

There was no getting out of it. True, he would be able to outrun the old wretches inside, but could he outrun his fears and years of being made fun of? If he didn't do it he would never live it down.

"Okay, keep a lookout." The words escaped his shivering mouth. *Just don't think about it. Get in and out quickly,* he repeated the thought to himself, leaving his school bag in Stephen's uncomfortably cold hands.

Quickly passing through a broken section of the fence, he glanced down the road towards home, hoping Trish wouldn't catch sight of him going into the forbidden territory.

Both onlookers held their breath as he slowly pushed his way through the knee-high weeds towards the building which would surely prove his bravery to the two boys, standing hunched over safely on the other side of the fence. Alan studied every crack in the rotted wooden door, waiting for the hinges to creak open at any moment. His breath was deep and shallow and he fought with himself to keep moving forward.

Following another few steps towards the creepy

cesspit, he eyed the old, mouldy net curtains flowing hauntingly in the windows, no doubt due to the years of disrepair on the old wooden window frames struggling to keep the stained glass upright.

As he reached the first window, he quickly glanced into the darkness contained inside, and found nothing. He turned towards Steven and Anthony, who were well hidden behind the scattered wild hedging entangled around other weeds and fence.

Typical! He thought to himself, ducking beneath the windowsill and shuffling across, trying not to get too wet from the soggy ground, to the next window. He held his breath in an effort to calm his pounding heart and peeked inside once more. Again, he was greeted by complete blackness.

"Well, do you see anything?" One of the boys shouted from the road. If Alan would have been beside Stephen, he would have answered with a punch due to being such an idiot for giving him away.

However, convinced no one was home, he stood to his feet.

"They're not home," he said back. Not too loudly though, just in case.

Alan then approached the ominous front door, whilst the boys ducked back into position again. Stepping onto the beaten, broken concrete steps, every leg muscle was like a coiled spring, ready to release to safety at a moment's notice. He tried the door handle which was unsteady and moved almost too freely, but the door was locked. Definitely another good indication that the house was vacant. Turning back to the road, he shrugged his shoulders.

Anthony motioned him to go around the back.

Just a quick look, he thought, rounding the house to reveal an equally overgrown, dank environment.

Alan quickly took in the wide back garden/dumping ground and old chain, collar, and dog house where Frank used to keep his dog, which had been dead quite a few years. He then spotted one of the old cottage sliding windows was left open. Of course, he immediately assumed it was to allow the stench of death to escape the house. He slowly approached the window, as the wind pushed on his back. Looking inside, he couldn't identify anything drastically out of the ordinary. Maybe the duster could have been used a bit more, but other than that observation, everything else seemed normal.

Imagine what they would think if I open the front door and step out through it, they aren't home so what harm could it really do? I'll be quick. He thought to himself as the adrenaline began to flow through him. Without a second thought he squeezed his slim body through the rattling window and into the house.

The smell of old age and dampness filled his nostrils. After a brief moment, his eyes adjusted to the murkiness inside. He stood within a small room containing an old twin-tub washing machine and a rickety wooden clothes horse. He then looked towards the room door, half-closed, swaying gently in the breeze trespassing alongside him. Reaching for the door, he gritted his teeth, pulling it slowly open. Stepping slowly into a dimmer room connecting the sitting room and kitchen, unease came over him. He glanced around the area and couldn't identify anything out of the ordinary; no butchered animals on the kitchen counter, no jars of human teeth standing on the shelves, and no decomposing human remains nailed to the floor. In fact, all things taken into consideration, it was a perfectly normal house needing some general maintenance.

Moving through the black room, he bumped his foot on a stereotypical small table camouflaged within the obscurity.

"Fuck sake!" he cursed himself. He waited for an old disgruntled voice to ask what the hell he thought he was doing, but no words other than his own broke the silence.

Aided by the thin sliver of light defiantly beating its way into the room, he began to make his way to the front door. He noticed two closed doors, one to his left and one to his right. He knew the one to his right was the room where Stephanie carried out her sessions and he assumed that the other lead to their bedroom. So he assumed the one he just broke into must have been Michael's old bedroom, converted into a rather poor attempt at a utility room. Thoughts of the dead boy sent an almost paralysing shiver up his back, and he somehow felt like he had desecrated the room.

Panic stricken he headed for the door. It was

then he saw the trap door in the rotting wooden floor, a little to his right. *I've always wondered why people go into places like that in horror movies, and now here I am wanting to look.*

Taking a deep, nervous breath, he walked towards the door, noticing that the latch on it wasn't locked. It creaked open. It was impossible to see anything through the darkness, and of course all he could think of was being pushed into the dank hole from behind, locked in and left to rot.

Alan reached into his pocket and took out his phone to help fight back some of the overwhelming darkness. He decided to have one quick glimpse and then get the hell out of there. He slowly tip toed onto the rickety, old wooden stairs then began his descent into hell. Every hair on his neck stood as a bead of sweat ran along his cold, right cheek. With his phone outstretched in front of him, he had to continually press the *on* button to keep the phone illuminated.

The steps buckled under his weight as he stared at the couple of inches of the room lit in front of him. Reaching the bottom of the stairs, he shone the phone around quickly, not recognising anything glaringly obvious. Meanwhile, outside the two boys shivered in the growing wind.

"What the hell is taking him so long? Should we go in after him?" Stephen asked.

Without any warning, a loud, painful boy's scream echoed from within the condemned house.

Chapter 8

The two stunned boys looked at one another other with terror incised on their pale faces. Neither knew exactly how to react. Those crazy bastards had just captured their friend, and what could they do about it? If they went in to save him, they would be captured too.

"Quick, we better go get Dad," Anthony stuttered, running his way down the isolated road towards home. Stephen was close behind, he didn't care about leaving their bags on the ground.

They were hammering the front door moments later, and a disgruntled Declan answered the door, wiping food from the side of his mouth.

"Dad, the Moore's have Alan!" Stephen shouted, as he pointed up the road towards where the boy was currently being tortured to no end. The man's eyes and mouth widened with shock as a dry canvas painted its way across his tongue.

"Okay, go get Daniel." He shut the door then made his way towards a building he had never admitted to being scared shitless of, and even more so, the monsters dwelling within it. Stepping closer, he couldn't help but feel less macho, requesting back up to confront people who were surely well into their eighties.

It wasn't long until Daniel and Trish came frantically running up the road, not knowing the condition of their son. Owen and Amy were close behind.

Quickly passing Declan, Daniel ran straight to the door to hell and began beating on it viciously.

"Let me fucking in!" he roared as Trish joined her concerned husband.

There was no answer.

"Okay stand back." He kicked the ancient door in. He entered without a second thought and was followed closely by his wife, Owen, Amy, and lastly by Declan. The two teenagers remained at the gate to the property.

Every single ounce off Trish's heart sank as she spotted some blood on the floor.

"Jesus, Daniel. What have they done to him?" she said, pointing him to the red fluid coming from the trap door, trailing across the floor towards a room in front of them.

Daniel ran and pulled open the door. More scattered red splotches lay on the floor inside. Their eyes couldn't cope with the unknown horror of their son's demise. Trish quickly looked away. Owen gestured to Amy to bring her outside.

The front door squeaked open behind them, and in walked Frank and Stephanie Moore.

"What are you doing in here?" a raspy, grumpy old man's voice asked.

Daniel shot across the room, not taking notice of

the old table he overturned along the way, and grabbed Frank by the scruff of the neck. "Where is my son, you sick fuck?"

"Stop," Stephanie screamed, quickly coming to her husband's aid, placing her feeble hands on Daniel's shoulder in an effort to restrain him. He easily shrugged her worthless attempts away without difficulty.

"What the hell are you talking about?" Frank asked, nostrils flaring, trying to catch his breath. He grabbed Daniel's hands to try and ease the roughness of the interrogation. Everyone else watched on without saying a word.

"You know what the fuck I'm talking about! Where is he?" Daniel said, spittle sprinkling his lips.

Again Stephanie made an attempt to break up the one-sided fight. The irate man turned his attention to her once more, he quickly released Frank and shoved her away. Meanwhile, Frank lost his footing, fell backwards, and smacked the back of his fragile head off the solid tile fire place. Blood gushed from the indented wound. Stephanie jumped to his side and frantically patted him on the chest awaiting a response.

"Quick, somebody help him!" she pleaded as the tears saturated her face. Looking around at the motionless spectators, to her, time had grinded to a halt. No immediate help was coming, and her stomach clenched.

"Please, Frank, wake up."

Those words and the drastic scene unfolding in front of Amy's softening eyes prompted her to reach for her phone and she dialled 999. Daniel stood there; firstly, wondering where they had his son, and secondly, how the fuck did the old bastard end up on the ground dying.

"Where the fuck is my son!" Trish roared without a care in the world.

"I don't know, and I don't fucking care." An emotionally devastated elderly woman screamed back, as she cradled Frank in her warm, blood soaked arms.

Daniel turned to Amy, who was speaking with the ambulance crew already on route to the scene and then turned back to the man dying in front of him.

"You all saw it right? He just fell," he stuttered, swallowing a lump of saliva down his dry throat.

"Yeah, we know, Daniel. Don't worry," Owen said, placing a hand on his shoulder.

The supportive words fell on deaf ears, whilst Daniel pondered what horrors his son had been subjected to. He felt sick to the bone knowing he still hadn't found him. Without further thought, he pulled the old, wobbly furniture aside, and darted back to the room they were about to investigate before they were interrupted.

Looking around the room, he found no lingering evidence of trouble apart from the blood drying before him.

Owen followed him to the room and said, "Daniel, come on. We can't do this, and the guards are probably on the way here too. We have already broken into the place and we'll have a lot of explaining to do if they see us doing this with Frank the way he is."

Meanwhile, Frank grew paler, and Stephanie's cries grew louder on the cold floor. None of the onlookers had planned things to turn out like that.

"Are you fucking serious? I need to find Alan. He could be dead somewhere in this shithole," he snarled back, shrugging Owens hand off his shoulder.

Daniel searched the inside of the abandoned room for any sign of his son—clothing, hair, signs of a struggle—but nothing could be found. Owen glanced towards the others, and Trish nodded to leave Daniel be and let him search.

We'll be brought out of here in handcuffs, he thought, turning back to the frenzied man in front of him.

Meanwhile, Frank's blood made its way around the floor. Declan stepped back a little to prevent it soaking the soles of his shoes. The sight of the advancing dark liquid made him nauseous. Amy approached to try and help Stephanie, and was met with opposition.

"Stay the hell away from us. You did this!"

Not wanting to fuel the fire any further, everyone remained where they were. Daniel's frantic search echoed through the silence between Stephanie's sobs.

"Where is he, Trish?" he cried, opening the door into Stephanie's spiritual reading room. He was greeted by a freezing chill and a gloomy, unsettling atmosphere. Stepping into the room, sirens pierced the country from a distance. Owen quickly ran to Daniel, grabbed him, and struggled to drag him from the room.

"Come on, we need to go outside," he said trying to restrain his friend fighting against him.

Daniel's eyes lit up when he saw a movement within the dark shadows in a corner of the room. He assumed it was his missing son, cowering with fear.

"Alan!" His voice boomed.

"He's not in there. Come on, let the guards find him. They'll be here in a minute." Owen continued dragging him back out through the door.

"I fucking saw him!" Daniel snapped as his face grew redder.

Declan joined Owen, and both escorted the irate man outside the house, still shouting his boy's name. Trish quickly joined them, and as she stepped outside the property, she threw a *'why the fuck did you call them?'* look at Amy. But Amy knew it was the right thing to do; a man was currently dying on the floor in front of her, and she would never forgive herself if she hadn't called.

"Stay there, guys," Declan told his sons peering into the garden.

Moments later, the wailing ambulance parked alongside the barely standing gate. A man and woman jumped out, blue emergency lights still blinking, and jogged towards the house carrying a large medical bag. They didn't bother stopping to speak with the trespassers taking in the scene unfolding in front of them.

"Those sick fucks have my son," Daniel said as they passed him into the house, surely about to be visited by death.

Stepping through the door, they were welcomed by a devastated woman and a pale faced, blue lipped man.

"They did this!" Stephanie said, rocking back and forth, holding her dying husband in her arms.

"Call the police," The male paramedic said to his colleague, sensing there was something more going on with the situation. The lady obliged, and he continued, putting the medic bag beside Frank then checked for a pulse. Frank's neck faintly popped against his fingers. He was alive, but barely holding on. Most of his blood had coated the floor. Pressure was quickly applied to the wound, followed by a number of whimpering groans.

The lady paramedic returned to the house and comforted Stephanie.

"Please save him, Siobhan," Stephanie pleaded, glancing at her name badge.

"Don't worry. We'll look after him," the young paramedic replied, aiding Stephanie outside to some well needed fresh air.

Inside, after some quick body assessments, a dressing and bandage were quickly applied to Frank's immobile head in an effort to plug farther fluid loss.

After what seemed like hours, a second set of

sirens echoed across the countryside as the Gardaí rapidly approached the scene. Again, a male and female stepped out of the second emergency vehicle. The female officer instructed everyone to remain where they were as she joined Siobhan and Stephanie. The male officer went inside to investigate the entire scene.

"Can you tell me what happened? Take your time," the Garda asked Stephanie, removing a black notebook and pen from her pocket. Siobhan then returned to the house to help treat Frank.

"We came home, and they had broken in. He grabbed Frank, and then he fell," she said, grasping for breath, pointing at Daniel.

"They have my son. He could be dead!" Daniel shouted, twitching with anger and struggling to keep control.

"Please, be quite. I'll be with you in a moment." The officer instructed.

"Please, can I go back into him?" Stephanie asked trying her best to rub the tears from her face with a quivering hand, watching Siobhan retrieve the stretcher from the ambulance.

"It's best you stay here. Let them look after Frank as quick as they can."

The door swung as the stretcher was pushed to the edge of the bland concrete steps, and then aided to the ground with the help of the male Garda. Stephanie quickly went to her husband's side. Holding his icy hand, she sensed that death already had its hold on him, and it was slowly tightening its grip. The stretcher was secured in place on the ambulance and Stephanie sat beside him praying. She didn't give a shit about anything else in the world. Nothing else mattered, only the current condition of her husband. She just wanted him to open his eyes.

"Okay, so what I've got already is that there was a forced entry, an argument, and there is an elderly man currently being rushed to hospital," the female officer projected to the nervously awaiting group. The uneasiness Daniel and Trish underwent was due to the fact that they still hadn't located their son.

"Names and addresses please," she added, jotting down the replies on paper which was splotched by the spitting rain.

Daniel said, "Officer, please, look inside. Our son is missing, and there is blood in a separate room in there. That's why we broke in."

"It's true. My sons said they had him," Declan said backing his friend up.

"What have those creeps done now?" Margret asked, throwing her venomous words into the mix. The Moore's nosy next door neighbour, stood beside the two dumb struck teenagers at the fence, wondering what all the commotion was about.

The Garda glanced towards the unsettled boys.

The other Garda joined the group and informed his partner about the blood along the floor and in the room, which Daniel had ranted about.

"Okay, we'll begin an entire search of the

property," the male Garda said, returning to the house. Meanwhile, the female officer quizzed the group further.

"So, tell me what happened?" she asked flicking to a fresh page on her notebook.

Daniel said, "The boys said they had my son. So, obviously, I wanted to find him before anything happened to him."

The Garda wrote more notes. Frowning, frustration crept its way across Daniel's face.

"The boys said that?"

"Yes officer, that's right." Declan said, confirming the information Daniel gave to the Garda.

"Just so I get this right; the boys told you an elderly couple had *got* your son, and you decided to march up here and break in without a second thought?" she said.

Trish didn't appreciate the Garda's snide remarks, which was clearly shown by her scrunched eyebrows and reddening cheeks. "Listen, Officer, our son is missing. They are fucking creeps, okay? We came up here, no one answered the door, so what were we supposed to do? Wait for you to get here? He could be dead by now, and all you want to do is write."

Those words caused the Garda to quickly glance up from the notebook.

"Careful now. You've already broken into a house, a man is currently on his way to the hospital, and we are still trying to establish exactly what happened here. My partner is inside searching the house as we speak. So, tell me how Frank ended up on the ground?"

Jesus Christ how fucking long is this going to take? Daniel thought, grinding his teeth to their breaking point.

Amy, on the other hand, still hadn't made eye contact with Trish. However, she was still relieved she called for help.

"We went in to try to find my son, and we found blood on the floor and in a room at the back of the house. There was no sign of him, and that's when they came home. So, I quizzed them."

"Were you physical?" the Garda countered.

"Yes, but not violently. I swear the man just slipped. I just want to find my son officer." Daniel started to crumble, his eyes moistening.

"Is this what happened?" she directed to the group.

"Yes, Officer. We all were there when it happened," Owen confirmed.

Stepping through the door once more, the male Garda shook his head towards his partner, indicating that he had not found the missing boy.

"Okay, what we are going to do now is launch a search for your son. Is there anywhere he could be?" the female Garda asked.

Trish thought, *if we knew that don't you think we'd already be looking there?*

"No idea," they replied in turn.

Absorbing Daniel and Trish's despair, the Garda showed the first ounce of compassion.

"Okay. Usually we'd be hauling you down to the station, but I have your details and you won't be going anywhere. The main thing is that we find your son, and it won't help having you all dragged in. The more sets of eyes we have looking for him, the better. I want you all down at the station tomorrow morning at 9am sharp so I can get an official statement of each one of you.

"I will also want to speak with your two sons," she said to Declan, who nodded in agreement. "Let's not take away from the fact that there was a break in committed here, and a man is severely injured. Our main goal now is finding your missing boy. He is not in the house, so we will sweep the surrounding area. Go home, and let us know if you think of anything that could help."

She then reached for her radio, spat some updates, and then returned to the squad car, as her colleague sealed off the area. In her passing, Margret asked what had happened, and she was instructed to stay out of it and return home. Moments later, the other Garda was in the car, and they headed back towards the station.

Entering the A&E department of the nearest hospital located forty minutes away, Frank's condition had worsened. His heart rate had dropped and his pulse had weakened even more. He was immediately transferred to the Intensive Care Unit. Stepping through the large white doors and witnessing her husband being connected to various machines and re-bandaged, Stephanie knew that the end was near and wondered how she could survive in the damning world alone. Filled with emptiness and hurt, she sat at his bedside and stared at the dying man.

Daniel cradled his sobbing wife in his arms as he himself struggled to contain the waterworks. He twitched uncontrollably wondering the horrific ends his son may have faced, and all he wanted to do was go out and look for him. However, he couldn't leave Patricia in the state she was in.

The Guards better find him soon.

"Where is he? What did they do to him?" Trish muttered as the salty liquid running down her face moistened her lips.

"I don't know love-"

The back door closed. Both parents turned, and to their amazement, standing in front of them, was a bloodied, mucky, wet, and breathless Alan.

Chapter 9

Daniel and Trish jumped to their feet and raced to their son, consuming him with hugs. Then they inundated him with questions like: "Are you okay?", and "What did they do to you?"

Alan stood there unresponsive.

"Alan, you're bleeding! What happened?" Daniel asked assessing his son and awaiting an answer.

"I need to sit down," he replied, squeezing past them to sit on the leather sofa. Usually, his mother would have roared at him to not sit down with filthy clothes on, but at that stage, couldn't give a shit. All she was concerned about was that was her son was home and she wanted to make sure he was okay.

"You need to get out of those damp clothes," she said, flicking on the kettle to make him a cup of chicken soup—his favourite.

"I will in a second. I need to talk to you first," the boy said through chattering teeth.

Concern bombarded the boy's parents once more as they joined him on the sofa.

"What is it son? What did they do?" Daniel queried.

"Is Frank okay? I saw him being taken away in the ambulance," the boy asked.

"There was an accident. He will be fine. Tell us

what happened?"

The boy took a long, hard, deep breath.

"They ... they didn't do anything."

"What do you mean? You're bleeding!" Daniel said, trying to make sense of the answer just given to him.

Alan's lower jaw began to quiver and tears trickled their way down his cold face.

"I ... broke in, Dad. They didn't do anything to me. They weren't even home."

Regret, guilt, confusion, and a sprinkle of anger sped into Daniel's mind as he sat back from his son trying to justify the answer.

"What the hell do you mean you broke in? Why are you bleeding?" Trish demanded.

"It was a dare. I climbed through a back window to look around. I then went down to the basement. It was too dark to see exactly where I was going, and I banged my leg off an old table, I think." The boy muttered.

Daniel thought of Frank and how he had accused him wrongfully. He felt pathetic, and worried for the first time about the condition of the elderly man.

"I shouted, and then climbed back out through the window as quickly as I could. When I got outside, Anthony and Stephen were gone, so I didn't know what to do. I was afraid, Dad. I really didn't know what to do, so I limped and hid in the field across the road trying to figure out what to do. Once I seen you all coming up the road, I wanted to come out but I was scared of what might have been said. I'm so sorry. I didn't want this to happen." The boy broke down, cradling his head in his hands.

Both parents were stunned. They exchanged glances while waiting for the other to react.

The click of the kettle turning off cut through the atmosphere. However, neither parent went to make the soup for their son.

"I can't believe this. We broke into that house looking for you, and you're the one who broke in in the first place. How the fuck are we going to explain this to the guards? It'll be even worse now!" Daniel said.

Trish felt the exact same as her husband, but she didn't bother adding to the scolding.

"Go get yourself cleaned up!" his father said.

The boy went to get a shower with his head hung low, fearing that, at any moment, the Guards would kick the front door open searching for him.

"How are we going to explain this tomorrow?" Trish asked, staring at Daniel, praying for an answer she hoped would somehow make the recent memories fade away.

"We can't say he broke in. He'll never get through the pressure of the questioning and he'll probably have a record. Imagine what his future will be like. What he did was completely stupid, and we will punish him, but we can't tell the Guards he broke in!"

Trish didn't answer, she just nodded in

agreement, knowing that what they had done was wrong and more so knowing that they had to put their son first.

Chapter 10

Stephanie clung to her husband's bedside waiting for any sign of improvement, but she knew his symptoms pointed in only one direction; the Grim Reaper eagerly awaited Frank to join him.

Looking at his closed eyes, she wondered what must be going through his mind, Steph reflected on how Frank use to always be concerned about her gift. One specific night came to mind. The night Trish tried to speak with her father and say goodbye properly.

"Are you okay, dear?" a raspy, tired man asked his wife as he entered the room to see if everything was ok, after the abrupt exit by the young girl.

"Yes, it was Natas again. He is becoming more resilient," Stephanie responded.

On many occasions, she had told him about the dark forces trying to break through, and Frank was becoming concerned by how much willpower and exertion the constantly bombarding fiend placed on her both mentally and physically.

"Why don't you quit all this?"

"Never. If I can help people put their minds at ease, I will, and I can't just turn this off."

"I know, my love." Frank cradled his wife's bruised hand in his own. "I just worry about you."

"I'll be fine." She said in that old, stereotypical *'don't worry about me* kind of way.' "I have encountered malicious forces before but none are like Natas. He seems to be evil incarnate but I can't let him break me. He has chosen to test me and if he finds a way into this world I'm terrified of what he would be capable of. I'll have to be more vigilant from now on."

Those words rested just as uneasily with Steph as much as they did with Frank. After all, even the strongest piece of steel breaks after continuous wear and tear.

Sighing deeply, clasping her husband's cold hand in the hospital bed, her mind was drawn to another memory ...

It was a number of nights following her and Trish's, terrifying encounter with Natas. She lay on the flat of her back, staring at the ceiling through immense layers of darkness. She was just about to nod off to sleep. However, before finally closing her eyes, she uncontrollably jumped in the bed. Her senses went on high alert. She knew that reflex was a reaction to someone (or something) being close by.

Raising to her elbows, she quickly looked around the room, eyes pulsating, so too did the shadows within it. Staring into the darkness, she had experienced so many times before, a spirit would sometimes pop by to say hello. Waiting for the spirit to make itself known, she glanced towards Frank comfortably sound asleep beside her. She then glanced towards a corner in the room and noticed two large, pale white eyes glaring back at her. Before she had any time to react, two deformed, monstrous, skin deprived hands lunged for her neck.

Gripping the unearthly hands, she called Frank.

"Set me free, you fucking bitch!" Natas roared. "You won't keep me locked away forever. I'll break you!" the demon said, tightening its grip and shaking her violently.

Gasping for air and looking into those eyes, Stephanie sensed countless years of pain, hate, and torment. She fought with all her strength to keep his inhuman hands at bay. If she broke, there would be no stopping him.

Frank awoke, switched on the bedside light, turned to his wife, and Natas returned to his dark infested pit. Stephanie rubbed her neck to try to relieve some of the pain.

"Are you okay? What happened?" he asked looking around the room and then towards his wife. His jaw dropped noticing the huge hand marks on her neck.

"Jesus, Stephanie. What did that to you?" he asked, feeling useless.

"I'm okay. Once he sees I'm not easily influenced, he'll eventually give up," she said, praying that she was right.

"Well, you know how I feel about this, and now I'm even more worried about Natas. Please, promise me that if he does anything like this again, you'll stop."

"Okay," Steph said, still massaging her aching neck.

Struggling to contain her rattling concern from her husband, she knew deep down that she couldn't stop. No matter even if she wanted to.

The swing of the chunky white hospital door as the doctor walked in brought Stephanie back to reality. He was tall and slender and wore the typical slacks, shirt, and tie combo. Frank was the only patient in the Intensive Care Unit, and as he walked their way, Stephanie eyed his name badge which read: Dr. O' Neill.

"Doctor, please, tell me he'll be okay?" Stephanie hoped turning towards him.

He acknowledged her with a smile and proceeded to check the man's barely evident pulse, the doctor also checked the drip he was connected to, and then the chart located at the foot of the bed which contained the initial assessments of the doomed individual.

"We're doing all we can to keep him comfortable, my dear." He rested a reassuring hand on her shoulder.

Stephanie knew exactly what those words indicated.

"How long does he have?"

"With the blood loss, his age, and the severity of the injury, I feel that it is only a matter of time before he passes. I'm very sorry."

Stephanie's mouth curled downwards even farther, as tears stung her eyes. *How many people's hearts has he snapped over the years with those words?*

"I know it's hard, but try and get some rest. We will keep you up to date on any developments," he added, before he left the room to tend to other patients.

As the door closed behind him, the beep of the heart monitor was her only company. Looking at her dying husband, she wondered again how she would survive.

About half an hour passed, and Stephanie found herself nodding off. The day's events had really taken their toll on her. Just before her eyes welded shut, she leaped in the hard, uncomfortable hospital chair.

Without warning "Steph ... an ... ie," was uttered slowly around the room in a deep, gritty voice.

She turned towards the doors, presuming it was someone entering the room, but they were firmly closed. No one was approaching her.

A chill made its way through the soles of her feet and up to her temple, which caused her to wince in pain. The bright lights within the room flickered sporadically.

Something was coming.

Her attention was lured to the drip feeding into her husband's body. The surface of the liquid quivered and then pin holes began to pop through it, releasing its contents onto the floor. She glanced towards the heart monitor, and its display was distorted by some interference. Stephanie held her ears as they filled with a mind-numbing ringing. A light bulb popped and it was then she noticed the enormous, inhuman shadow lurking behind one of the bedside curtains farther down the room.

"Hello?" she whispered, daring not to move an inch.

Her name was whispered in response.

Moments passed, and then the demonic creature stepped out from behind its cover. The blood drained from Stephanie's face as she witnessed the sight of Natas in his true form for the very first time in her life. He was approximately seven feet-tall and covered in blistered skin, which was a dark charcoal colour. Four cracked, worn horns stood proudly on top of his bald head, two long horns located at his forehead and two shorter ones in the rear. His *facial* features were made up of massive white eyes, two holes which she assumed was a nose, and mouth housing razor sharp teeth; some of which protruded passed his lips. He grinned at her, and she noticed his mouth was slanted from the right cheek down to the jawline.

She gripped the chair tightly as she watched him stepping forward. He had three arms. The right one was longer than the left and the other, located in the middle of his *chest,* was like a raptor's limb with three long claws dangling from it.

Darkness crept into the room as he moved through it. Fear abseiled its way down her spine, but she would not break. Her nostrils were filled with a horrid unearthly smell as he neared her. Her left arm quivered with a chill surrounding her.

Reminding herself to look at the demon that had manifested in front of her directly in the eye, she asked, "What do you want?"

Natas' head twitched.

"I've come to you to say let me in!" he finally hissed. "I've watched you all your life and witnessed all the pain, torment, and nasty comments made about you. I can make it all go away. All you need to do is take my hand."

Panic sprinted through her mind as he raised his left hand waiting for her to take hold.

"Look at what they did," he continued, acknowledging her husband lying beside her drawing on his last number of breaths. "Surely, you wouldn't let him die for nothing? Let me carry your pain. Take my hand."

Stephanie had become drowsy and couldn't determine if the creature had spoken the words out loud or if he had uttered them within her mind.

"Let me take your pain," he stated once more. "I will see to it that you will witness no more pain from this moment on, and I will ensure that all those involved with this will receive the same treatment you have been given," the beast grinned.

Glancing towards her dying husband, she thought, *Why should I protect them? Every single one of them should be lying here instead of Frank.*

Natas smiled wider, studying her thoughts.

"I can guarantee that it will happen." he added. "Just take my hand, and let me take care of it for you. They deserve everything that is coming to them."

Before she knew it, she found herself raising her trembling hand towards the monster in front of her. Years of being subjected to hate, name calling, exclusion, and blame was the motivation driving the terrified woman's hand upwards. Before reaching Natas' hand, a flashback of her son jumped to the forefront of her mind. She remembered his smile, carefree personality, and thought, *I can't do this to the other children in the area, a child needs its parents.*

Sensing her hesitation, Natas lunged forward and grabbed her hand.

"Come on, you fucking bitch. Its time! I told you, you couldn't keep me at bay forever. Now set me free or I'll tear you apart!" he roared in an unnatural voice.

A paralysing pain ran through her right arm to her shoulder, like she had been bitten by one hundred poisonous snakes. She tried with all of her feeble might to pull her hand away, but it was no use. He had latched onto her. She concentrated, as before, as hard as possible in an effort to *will* him away, but Natas just smiled at her worthless attempt.

"You're too weak. You can't do anything. Once I'm finished with you, I'm going to destroy everyone you ever had contact with. First, you. You have endless torture ahead."

91

He ripped her from the chair. Still holding her up by the hand—now above her head—her blood clotted feet tip toed the floor. She squirmed in panic, but nothing could overcome his unearthly power. Smiling at her, his longest limb raised from his side.

"Please," she uttered.

No attention was paid to her plea. The demon placed its large fingers into her mouth, and with the sound of one quick, violent click, her lower jaw was ripped from her face. Writhing in agony, he flung her violently against the solid wall. Her head fractured, and her lifeless body fell to the cold floor. Natas stretched his three arms, finally enjoying the freedom he had yearned for so long. After harvesting her soul, his evil attention was then drawn to Frank.

He stepped to the bedside and briefly looked at the already condemned man. He raised his large fist once more and delivered a crushing blow to Frank's skull, which caved in underneath the strike. Blood splattered the walls. Doctors raced into the room after the heart monitor flat lined, their mouths hit the floor followed by screams due to the horrific murder scene in front of them. Natas was gone.

Chapter 11

Bridgett was washing the dishes after the evening's dinner with Declan and the two boys.

"What the fuck happened over there today?" Declan asked, as he dried the dishes beside her.

Bridgett didn't answer. She just stared into the darkness coating the winter countryside, wondering how the old man was doing in the hospital.

She placed the last plate on the draining counter, the room fell into blackness.

"Great." Declan huffed, reaching into the drawer under the kitchen sink and pulled out a torch.

Bridgett glanced to the digital dial on the electric cooker, and it was dead too. She peered outside and spotted that the lights still glowed perfectly in Trish's house.

"Somethings wrong. The lights are still on next door." She pointed towards the brightness standing proudly amongst the darkness.

"A trip switch must be down," he replied, passing her through the kitchen then into the hallway to inspect the electrical power box above the front door.

Shining the torch, he quickly raised his eyebrows noticing that all switches were in the upright position.

"Go get the boys," Bridgett ordered.

Without hesitation, he marched upstairs to his sons. Reaching the top of the stairs, he noticed their bedroom door was closed, which was unusual, because neither of them were capable of staying still for two seconds.

"Boys," he called, knocking on the door.

No reply.

He opened the door and froze in his tracks, witnessing the two youngsters cowering in the corner of the room.

"What's wrong?" he asked, uncomfortably watching his sons grow paler every passing second.

No words were spoken. Stephen raised a shaking hand towards the dark corner behind the door Declan stood beside. He shone the torch around the door. A dark figure moved towards him and slammed the door shut with such force the wood cracked in half. Declan was thrown backwards, falling hard onto the floor.

"What was that?" Bridgett roared, racing up the stairs.

"Stay back," Declan said, pulling his heavy, aching body up from the floor. "There is someone in the room with them."

Fear crashed over Bridgett. She couldn't establish if she had heard him correctly, or if he was confused after his fall.

"What do you mean?" she said stepping forward.

Turning to her, holding his neck, the blood drained from his face, witnessing the monstrous figure lurking behind her.

"Behind—"

She screamed as Natas grabbed her and picked her up like a paperweight, smiling towards her shell-shocked husband. He flung her over the banister. She hit the ground with an almighty thud, fracturing her left ankle and hip.

"You bastard! I'll fucking kill you!" Declan roared, running towards the unknown evil in front of him.

With his left hand, Natas latched onto the pathetic man's shoulder.

"You have no idea how fucking pitiful you all are. The very smell of you makes me sick. Now, do the only thing you can do … die!" Natas growled.

He raised his enormous right hand, engulfing Declan's head. The man screamed as the demon slowly increased the pressure to his skull. Blood oozed from his ears followed by numerous vicious clicks and cracks as Declan's head caved in. Before he allowed his limp body to fall to the ground, Natas delivered a punch to Declan's face.

"DECLAN?" Bridgett screamed, following the commotion upstairs. She crawled towards the stairs, but stopped when she spotted the dark figure glaring at her at the top. The beast disappeared and then reappeared directly in front of her.

"What are you? This is the work of the Devil!" she said.

"The Devil?" he said, words clipped. "I'm *nothing*

like him. He was once an angel. I never held that title! I live in the darkness. Always have and always will!"

"Please, leave us alone. Boys get out of the house," she called, quickly trying to crawl away from the fiend in front of her.

Natas approached her and placed a clawed foot onto her delicate neck. Blue faced, and coughing, she made one final plea for her life. Ignoring her, he pressed down slowly, suffocating the life out of her.

Standing beside another dead body, Natas turned and looked towards the room where the two boys where still shitting themselves. He grinned, and was once again gone.

Chapter 12

"What a day eh?" Owen said, joining Amy on the large sofa in front of the TV.

"I know. Unbelievable," she said, as he placed his arm around her stressed shoulders.

"I know they're weird and all, but, Jesus, Dan fucking lost it up there. I suppose he is worried about Alan. I feel bad for not helping look for him, but I think I need to look after my own family first," he said, as he slightly tightened his grip around his love.

"I know what you mean. You can go if you want. I'll stay here with Christina if you like?" she said turning to him.

"No I'll ring him soon to see how he is doing. I'm sure he has enough to deal with. I just hope they find Alan safe and well," he replied.

"Me too."

A half an hour passed as the couple watched TV, and the darkness had fully enclosed the countryside.

Owen reached into his pocket and pulled out his mobile phone. After dialling the numbers, he waited for Daniel to answer.

"Hello, how are you now? Any word on Alan?" he asked, turning the volume down on the flat screen. Amy listened in closely beside him.

"Okay. Well, I hope they find him. Ring me if

you need anything, and let me know if you hear any news okay?" Owen said moments later, before he hung up.

"No word then?" Amy asked.

"No, nothing yet."

Three sharp, ear shattering knocks arrived at the front door, which caused Owen to jump. Amy giggled at his uneasiness. He frowned in response. Christina came from her room to answer the individual beating the crap out of their front door.

Opening the door, she was greeted by the fresh country air, surprised to find no one standing in front of her.

"Who is it?" Owen shouted to her.

"Nobody," she quickly replied.

Three more loud knocks echoed through the house. This time, from the back door.

"Someone's acting the bollox now!" Owen grunted, standing from his comfort, then quickly walking towards the door. A person stood behind it, who was moments away from getting a punch in the face. Pulling down hard on the handle, he swung the door open. Owen was amazed to find no one standing on the step either. Without any time to react, three thunderous knocks came from upstairs.

"That's it," Owen bellowed, running upstairs.

"Be careful," Amy nervously said after him.

Reaching the landing, the two doors downstairs slammed shut with violent bangs, followed by sadistic, evil laughter echoing around the house.

"Owen?" Amy called. Christina stepped over to her side.

"There must be a window open up here. That's why the doors slammed," he said. "Stay there. I'm going to see where this laughing is coming from.

"It's inside the house, Dad," his daughter said.

"Can't be. No one got past us. It's just someone playing a prank, and it won't be funny if I find them."

Slowly moving along the hallway, he found himself anxious and thought, *what would I do if I find someone up here?*

As he reached for the handle on the closed bedroom door, the lights died.

"Dad!" Christina called out, viewing a huge figure lunging at her mother from the darkness.
The figure shot into Amy and sent her viciously crashing against the solid wall behind her. Owen raced downstairs and joined his daughter at his wife's side. He reached into his pocket and pulled out his phone, using the light from its screen, he illuminated Amy's face.

"What the hell happened? Are you okay?" he asked, staring at her expressionless face. Looking closer, he noticed her eyes were murky. Amy giggled in a deep voice beside them. Owen and Christina looked at each other bewildered. Their attention quickly snapped back to Amy as her head contorted and clicked sharply in front of them.

"Mam?" her concerned daughter asked as shivers climbed her spine.

"You really have no fucking idea do you?" a male's voice growled from the woman's mouth. "I've taken her soul, and I'll soon have yours!"

The two looked on in horror whilst the possessed woman bit down hard enough her teeth snapped. She then laughed loudly, as the blood gushed to the floor she lay on.

A loud thump echoed from the kitchen. The pair spun to find nothing and quickly turned back to find Amy gone.

"What the—?" Owen muttered.

"Dad, I saw something."

Footsteps pounded their way through the darkness, towards the kitchen. Christina tightly gripped her father's arm.

"What's wrong with her?" the shaking girl whispered.

"Stay here."

Owen stood then made his way towards the adjoining kitchen devoured with shadow. Lifting his phone in front of him, he tried to navigate his way through the alien environment.

"Dad," Christina whispered.

He turned and shushed her. Footsteps made their way through the room once more. His attention was drawn to the clunking and clanging tin by the kitchen sink. Silence collapsed into the room as he struggled to traverse the dark environment to where the noise came from. Moments later, he eyed the glistening, scattered pots and pans. Next to them, a dark, juddering silhouette faced away from him.

"Amy" he whispered, stepping forward cautiously towards her.

There was no response. From behind, she seemed like a stranger to him. Nothing about her seemed familiar.

With only a number of small steps between them, he sensed her sharp, shallow, irregular breathing.

"Amy, are you okay?" he asked once again, as Christina stared on at the dismal, quivering, light coming from the phone moving farther away from her.

Reaching Amy, he peered around her right shoulder, his eyes widened and his jaw went slack. Amy's eyes were rolled to the front of her brain, while she faced the ceiling. The horror intensified when he looked down to see her cutting chunks of her arm off with a large carving knife.

"Amy, what the fuck—"

She screamed uncontrollably as Natas left her body and dove deep into Owen's soul.

Coming to her senses, Amy held her agonising wound, wondering where the last five minutes disappeared to.

The possessed man reached for the knife and then repeatedly stabbed her stomach.

"Now, die bitch," he snarled. Amy gulped for air and tried to figure out why her husband was killing her.

Upon hearing the struggle, Christina raced to her mother's aid.

"Dad, what are you doing?" she shouted, while grabbing his shoulders in a panic trying to save her mother's life. Natas shrugged her off with ease, then forced the knife hard into Amy's mid-section. The blade smashed her spine and exited through her back.

The possessed man turned to his petrified daughter, lifted his t-shirt, put the blade to his flesh, and cut deep from left to right. Natas left the room, and Owen fell to the ground beside his wife. The piercing pain was the first thing that sped through Owen's body. He didn't know which pain hurt more: the grief of viewing his lacerated, dead wife beside him, or the soreness of the open wound spilling bodily fluids and contents of his stomach to the floor around him.

"Jesus, what happened?" he uttered as he tried to pull the skin together.

"You killed her, Dad," his daughter said, tears streaming along her face.

He turned to his wife in disbelief. His bloody hands fell to his side as his life left his body.

Christina sobbed uncontrollably on the cold, blood-soaked floor. She tried—however, unable—to rationalise what had happened. One thing was certain, her parents were dead, and her heart—her entire soul—had been smashed to pieces.

Natas lived off fear, enjoyed torturing people, and wasn't going to stop until he had his fill.

Chapter 13

Switching off the bedroom light, Daniel climbed underneath the blankets with his wife.

"Seriously, how are we going to explain this tomorrow?" Trish asked, turning to him.

"I don't know, but we'll think of something," he replied.

However, the lump in his throat, and increasing feeling of gloom slowly moving over him, indicated otherwise. As Daniel stared at the dark ceiling, he was thankful that there was still several hours until they had to explain what happened at the Moore's house.

Eventually, the pair drifted off to a restless sleep.

While dreaming, Trish stood on a cold, dank, windy hillside. Staring into the swirling fog below, a dark figure approached her. Squinting to identify who it was, she was startled to realise that it was Stephanie, the woman of her nightmares approaching her. The harsh wind beat against her delicate face as she stepped backwards through the drenched weeds.

"Please, wait! I need to talk to you." The wind carried the haunting words to Trish's freezing ears.

She paused, noticing the concern in her voice. The old woman slowly stumbled her way to Trish.

"This is going to sound crazy, but you're in terrible danger. In fact, a lot of your friends are already dead," the woman said.

"What?" Trish said, unnerved.

"I set him free. Jesus, forgive me. I set him free!"

"Set who free?" Trish asked, watching the sadness grow in the dead woman's eyes.

"Evil," she responded. "He was tormenting me for years, and tonight, he finally broke me. I was so angry with what happened to my dear Frank. In some way, I may have unknowingly summoned this evil upon us."

Trish's confusion grew.

"It's a demonic force, Trish. He killed me, my husband, and is working his way through your friends towards you and Daniel."

Trish gasped. "What? why?"

"I don't have an answer to that. All I know is that he is coming, and I don't know if he can be stopped."

"So why warn me then?" she asked, snarling the words at the old woman.

"Because, so far, he hasn't harmed any of the teenagers who have seen this foul, unholy beast, and I know Alan is safe. I'm trying to help."

Seconds later, the elderly woman vanished and Trish awoke to blackness.

What a fucking nightmare! Her thoughts then went to the uncomfortable feeling from her thighs and back against the cold, damp blankets. This coldness was almost counteracted by warm urine as a loud bang echoed from downstairs.

"Daniel," she quickly said, as she shoved him to life.

"What?" He groaned, reluctantly turning to her.

"I think someone is breaking-"

Another thud crashed through the house, which brought Daniel quickly to his bare feet.

"Who the fuck is that?" he said.

"Stay there," he said, making his way slowly to the slightly opened door.

Pulling the door open, Alan greeted him, shivering on the landing, wondering, like his father, what the fuck was going on?

Both made their way downstairs, towards the forbidden darkness. Daniel didn't bother telling Alan to stay put because he knew his words would've have fallen on deaf ears. Instead he tried his utmost to contain his apprehensiveness for the sake of his son, who stayed close behind him.

Flicking on the light at the bottom, it rapidly beat back the night. Not a single item seemed out of position. Astonished due to the viciousness of the bangs, Daniel decided to investigate further. He switched on the outside light over the back door. No one stood in front of them.

A loud pop followed by a smash packed their ears as the kitchen light bulb exploded. Daniel turned to his left and found the incredibly large figure standing within the shadows in the corner of the room. He froze, seeing his son standing closer to the dark being. The dark figure lunging for his son and ripping him to pieces stampeded through his mind.

Before he had the opportunity to warn Alan, the light bulb outside the back door burst. Daniel turned again, finding nothing! He quickly spun towards the corner, and Natas was gone.

Upstairs, in darkness, Trish sat rigid on the mattress.

"Daniel," she called "What's going on?"

He replied but she couldn't clarify what he said. Scuffling across the mattress in an effort to hear better, she heard a low growl crawling from beneath the bed. She stiffened, remembering the contents of her nightmare, not trying to give away her position on the bed. She breathed as slowly as possible, anxiously trying to identify any other strange noises within the room.

Without any warning, a grotesque hand reached from underneath the bed and latched onto her leg. Her smooth skin darkened, blistered, and burned. She kicked and screamed. The hand returned to the shadows and an unnerving laughter ricocheted off the walls. She leaped from the bed and headed for the door, she ran downstairs into Daniel's arms, trying to ignore the stinging pain working its way along her left leg.

"What happened?" Daniel asked, unable to comfort his wife.

"Something is up there."

All three looked towards the top of the stairs and were horrified to witness a figure looking back at them.

"Let's get out of here!" Daniel said, feeling like a coward.

Swinging open the front door, the rain blasted against Alan's face, aided by the strong wind howling behind it.

"Run," Daniel shouted.

Alan turned as Natas reached for his father.

"Dad!"

Natas sank his unholy claws into Daniels chest with ease. Natas then swung for Trish. Daniel side-stepped, shielding his wife, and took the blow, which smashed his ribs to pieces. One jagged fragment burst its way out through Daniels side. He roared, pain fuelling his voice. Daniel shoved Trish away as best he could.

"Get out of here." His voice gurgled.

He turned his attention back to the demon. Natas picked Daniel off the ground. Trish peered on, stunned. His slanted teeth riddled mouth grinned at her. He then viciously slammed the man's weakened body to the floor. She helplessly watched as the unearthly force clawed violently at Daniel's back.

"Run," he said, wheezing each painful breath.

Natas placed a hand on the back of Daniel's head and pressed down. He squirmed for air as his nose was the first to break against the hard floor beneath him. Natas continued pressing. The beast crushed his entire face, killing him. Trish screamed, witnessing the diabolical scene.

Alan sprung into her mind. She turned and was welcomed by complete darkness. She started along the saturated footpath but was tripped, her left leg snapped in half.

Turning to face her ultimate end,

"Where were you the night I died?" said a voice she hadn't heard in several years.

Staring at the blackened doorway, her father stared at her. He stepped out from the doorway, older than the day he died, and walked as though someone constantly kicked him in the lower back.

"Dad?" she asked, unsure of how to react.

He was dressed in the same hospital gown he wore the night she and her mother identified his cold body in the morgue. She noticed the old, shaking, feeble man's mouth trying to rustle up more words. She moved towards him in disbelief. The pain from the snapped leg distracted her from the emotional anguish her father brought.

"I'm in Hell, I've seen no light," he continued, looking towards the damp, cold ground. "Everything is a lie. There is no hope after death."

Trish reached to him, and he giggled uncontrollably. He slapped her hand away with a dismissive swipe.

"Stupid fucking bitch! You see how pathetic your race is? One simple memory recall and you're a broken piece of shit, just like that!"

Trish didn't have time to react. Her *father* lunged at her and gripped her neck. She gasped for air while clawing at her father's face. He laughed, shaking his head rapidly from side to side, as the blood flowed from his face. Trish's eyes widened farther as he applied more pressure. One final squeeze, and a crunch sounded as her throat collapsed.

Meanwhile, Alan hid in the heavily overgrown ditch across the road. The rain hammered against him, he fought hard to contain his cries of pain, watching his parents being brutally murdered. The elderly man stood over the boy's mother admiring his work. Many times he watched a horror movie saying to himself, *If that was me, I'd do this and that*. But when in reality, he realised that he could all but sit frozen in position.

He, of course, didn't recognise the demonic manifestation as his grandfather, because Peter had died many years before he was born and he was barely recognisable compared to the family pictures Alan had been shown.

The man cast those dark, evil consumed eyes towards the boy cowering amongst the weeds and briers. The demon smiled at him and whispered, "See you soon."

Then he was gone, leaving the boy in complete disbelief.

Chapter 14

After the deaths, the Gardaí launched a massive investigation. First, they questioned the hospital staff and teenagers separately to establish what happened and to put together the identity of the murderer. Naturally, each story was completely different and more shocking than the last. The forensic examination of the properties provided no results and the post-mortem examination on the violently battered bodies didn't find anything other than the blatantly obvious; they were murdered in the most inhumane manner in the history of the area, and Christina's father had killed Amy then turned the knife on himself.

After the bodies were released from the hospital, the funerals were held. Following that mental bombardment, therapy was provided to the teenage survivors.

During the weekly sessions, Christina vividly recalled the distress in her father's eyes, taking in the sight of his beloved wife lying dead beside him as blood poured from his stomach.

"There was something else in the house that night!" she said firmly to the therapist, who looked like she had just finished college the week before.

"You've went through a traumatic experience,

and I'm sure a lot of things don't seem clear right now." Was the frustrating response.

I know what I fucking saw. The words dangled on the tip of her tongue, but instead she said "My Dad wouldn't have done that."

"Things may seem a little confusing now," the therapist replied, resting both hands on her crossed knee, leaning forward. "But in time, the hurt will sooth and all will become clearer."

You studied a degree for this? Was the answer Christina wanted to throw at her but instead she remained quiet and nodded.

Most of the other sessions conducted with the other teenagers reflected various, unbelievable stories from the events of that night.

Stephen said, "Something non-human was in our house. My brother and I saw it. It viciously killed our parents and vanished."

The investigation within the hospital provided no information either. It was a bloodbath, and no one was seen coming or going. Even the CCTV camera had been disabled in the room where the murders occurred.

The Gardaí had no leads to go on. They ordered another forensic investigation and a search of the scenes and nearby areas, but all proved pointless. They had no positive ID to go on in relation to the killer, unless the large, shadowy, clawed, demonic figure description from the teenagers was anything to go on.

The crimes couldn't be explained, and the cases remained open, leaving the community wondering what happened and if it was safe to live there or go out at night, or during the day for that matter.

Chapter 15

Over the next number of years, Alan spent time living with close friends of the family. He got by as best as possible considering what he had gone through. When he tuned twenty, he returned home, and spent most of his time physically and mentally piecing together what happened on the night his parents were taken from him. His everyday life wasn't improved, of course, living in the house where the murders took place. He realised that time was not a healer, but rather allows more questions and self-criticism to creep their way into daily life.

He kept contact with Stephen, Anthony, and Christina. But, eventually, they moved on with their lives. Christina moved abroad to live near family members, Stephen married a girl from Wicklow, and Anthony followed his pursuit of travelling Europe, funding for this was aided by renting out their parents' house. Anthony had some guilt with that, but he concluded there was no point in rotting away in some corner. Stephen was the person who encouraged him to go clear his head. Returning home, Anthony eventually got a job, a girl, and set up residence in Dublin.

Alan learned life and time mixed alongside your mind could do one of two things: further seclude him from society; or, after some time, he would begin interacting with people again.

He cautiously found himself venturing back into society, like a tame animal reintroduced into the wild. The first number of interactions included sideward glances, people timidly asking how he was doing, and the common, "Let me know if there is anything I can do."

Alan wondered if people said that truthfully or to make themselves—rather than him—feel better. How would they react if he actually called on them for help? He, of course, certain they would instantly regret their offer.

After some time, a pretty brunette walked into his life. Rebecca was from Cork, and had moved to the area to find work. Alan quickly fell for her. Her big blue eyes, heart-warming smile, slim figure, and bright personality made the fall easier.

He didn't beat around the bush to ask her out. Witnessing the slaughter of his parents taught him to seize every opportunity.

The two went out for some time before they took the next step. Rebecca agreed to move in with him.

Life fell into some sort of normality for Alan, and he slowly began to get some form of enjoyment out of it.

Chapter 16

Four more years passed, and Alan knew that the deaths of his parents would never be answered in a way which he could understand, and he would never be able to comprehend what he saw moments before his parent's deaths.

As he lay in bed, the alluring aroma of a fried breakfast glided its way upstairs into the bedroom, filling his nostrils. Almost tasting the rashers in his watering mouth, he submitted to temptation. He swung his legs from the bed, wiped his eyes, dressed, and then went down stairs to the kitchen.

Stepping through the door, he was greeted by the welcome sight of a plate on the table, holding fried sausages, rashers, pudding, a fried egg, and beans.

Rebecca turned to him and smiled. "It's about time you got up."

"I couldn't stay up there any longer. This smells lovely," he said, smiling and rubbing his hands together.

She stepped from the cooker, brought the frying pan over to his plate, and placed another sizzling egg next to the other.

"You really know how to look after me," he said approaching her and kissed her on the cheek.

She smiled and then sat at the other end of the

table. Alan joined her at the opposite side.

"Are you not having anything?" he asked, placing a juicy slice of rasher into his mouth.

"No, I'm fine thanks. Listen, I need to talk to you," she said as her bottom lip quivered.

Alan swallowed the food and sat back. "Is everything alright?"

"I had rehearsed so many times this morning, but now I can't remember how I even began the speech." She shifted uneasily in the seat then said, "I'm pregnant."

Alan almost turned the table over, jumping to his feet. "Are you serious?"

"Yes, I'm sure."

"Oh my God, I can't believe it," he said at the top of his lungs. He ran to her and smothered her with hugs. "You're sure?"

He pulled away, carefully placing both hands on the sides of her face.

"Yes, I am." She said, unable to contain the smiles of joy.

Alan erupted with glee, almost hugged Rebecca to death. "I can't believe it."

"I didn't know how you would react," Rebecca said with a hint of relief.

"Trust me, this is the best news I have heard in some time. I couldn't be any happier."

Slight hurt crept into Alan's overworking mind. The next course of action should be to tell his parents the news but they were beneath the cold soil and decayed fossils of their former selves.

They would want you to be happy and not worrying about them, he told himself. Although hard to do, he pushed the thoughts of his battered, broken parents aside and concentrated on enjoying this life changing happiness with his soulmate. An uncontrollable twitch came over him at the thought of becoming a father. He hugged Rebecca once more then she sat back down at the table.

"We'll keep this to ourselves for the time being okay?" she said, wiping the tears of happiness from her cheeks.

"Why? I want everyone to know this."

"I'm not three months gone yet, and I don't want to jinx this," she replied, sitting in the chair. Although she wouldn't admit it, she wouldn't reveal that she was a believer in the three-month rule.

"Okay, I understand." Alan smiled. "I can't believe it."

Over the next few weeks the couple revealed the news to family and friends, beginning with Rebecca's parents. It didn't take long for the presents and best wishes cards to come flooding in.

"We're going to run out of space for these," Alan teased, trying to squeeze another card onto the mantel piece.

"Don't complain. It's good to know people care," Rebecca said, joyfully stepping into the bright sitting room.

Turning to her, Alan smiled, taking in her small

frame beginning to show the signs of a slight bump. He placed a hand on her stomach he said, "I'm so happy I found you, you've given me the best gift in life. You, and now a son or daughter. I love you so much."

"I love you too, Alan," Rebecca said as tears filled her eyes.

Alan leaned forward and kissed the girl who turned his life around.

Chapter 17

Ambulance sirens rang through the early morning dimness. As the vehicle negotiated the winding corners, it was harder to establish which was louder, the screeching of the tyres or the screams from Rebecca. She was over a month early, and the concern on Alan's face highlighted the importance of getting to the hospital as quickly as possible.

"Something's wrong. I can't have the baby yet," she roared through the oxygen mask while holding Alan's hand.

"Don't worry, you'll be fine. We're going to look after you," he replied, placing his free hand onto her forehead to try and reassure her.

Glancing at his other hand, it had turned dark purple from the grip being placed upon it by his partner. Glimpsing into the darkness outside, Alan privately prayed that everything would be okay, and they would receive a perfectly heathy baby.

As the ambulance rolled up to the A&E department, they were greeted by a doctor and two nurses who quickly brought Rebecca inside.

"Please look after her," Alan pleaded as the doctor instructed him to wait in the waiting room.

After some quick assessments, the decision was made to carry out emergency surgery. They rushed

Rebecca into the operating theatre while Alan lingered in morbid monotony wondering what the hell was going on.

After two and a half hours of mental torment, a doctor stepped into the waiting room holding a chart.

"Alan?" he called.

The worried man sprung to his feet, and almost flipped the uncomfortable, worn chair over.

"How is she? Is the baby okay? Can I see them?" Raced from the distraught man's mouth.

"Both individuals are doing fine, considering the earliness of the birth. I'm happy to tell you that you have a healthy baby boy."

Alan exhaled an enormous sigh of relief.

"We will need to monitor your son to ensure he is okay. I must tell you that we encountered some complications during the surgery, but for now, both are as well as can be expected. You can go in to see them. Just follow me."

As he stepped into the room, tears pushed their way down Alan's face as he witnessed the sight of Rebecca cradling their son. She was still a little groggy after the anaesthetic and post-surgery painkillers flowing through her system.

Time stopped as he viewed his child for the first time, wrapped in a white towel.

"Isn't he beautiful?" Rebecca said, rubbing the child's cheek.

"He's amazing. Are you okay?" Alan replied, resting his arm around her, and the other hand beside hers holding their son.

"I'll be fine. I'm just happy this little one is okay." She smiled.

A wave of fulfilment and happiness washed over him. He didn't know how to react to the feeling overload, so he just sat back and enjoyed the proud moment.

The child lay content, eyes closed, and then muttered, relishing the comfort. Both parents turned to each other and smiled.

"Have you thought of a name for him yet?" Alan asked.

"No. I had so many favourite names picked before today, but now looking at him, none of them seem to suit him."

"I know what you mean," Alan said, moving closer to his family.

Rebecca looked at him adoring his son for a moment and then asked, "How about Daniel?"

Alan turned to her wide-mouthed. He couldn't believe she had suggested his father's name for their son. Tears built up in his already watered eyes once more.

"Are you sure?" he asked, shaking slightly.

"Of course. I know how much you loved them, and I'm sure Daniel would be proud to have his grandson named after him."

"It's perfect. I love you so much." Alan carefully leaned across and kissed her.

Following some close observation over the next

week, the pair were discharged from the hospital to a warm welcome home by Alan and close friends. The well-wishers, of course, left early that evening to allow mother and son to get some well needed rest.

"You go ahead with him. I'll turn off everything down here," Alan said later as he began to lock the doors and turn off the lights.

Moments later, he joined Rebecca in the bedroom, who was already fast asleep.

He approached the white cot at the end of the bed. He grinned, peeking over the wooden frame, looking at Daniel asleep within the warm, fluffy bedding, wondering to himself what he was dreaming about. Stepping away, he felt happy; unlike any other feeling he had experienced over his lifetime.

Chapter 18

Daniel had turned five years old. By then, he had already began convulsing violently at least once a month. These fits would usually occur in the early hours of the morning and last anywhere from a few seconds to minutes. Many times, Alan heard the loud *thump*, and would spring from the bed to rush into Daniel's room to find him on the floor shaking uncontrollably. While Alan cradled his son in his arms, he often felt helpless watching his jaw jerk out of alignment and eyes roll to the back of his head.

Rebecca and Alan regularly took him to the hospital for tests and check-ups and they were still far from an explanation to the cause behind the child's ill health.

"So what news do you have for us?" A frustrated mother asked the doctor sitting across the old, wooden table in front her.

"We are running tests at the moment."

Same old answer, Alan thought.

"Listen, Doctor, we've been coming here for almost a year and we are still no closer to an explanation. Just medication that doesn't seem to be working." Alan hissed.

"It's a complicated matter. We have carried out various neurological tests, and we still have not identified exactly what is causing Daniel to have so many seizures."

Both parents did not know how to take the answer.

"Well, how much longer do we have to put Daniel through this?" Rebecca asked.

"I wish I could give you a definite answer, but I can't. As I said, all test results have come back perfect. I'm baffled as to the cause. Take comfort in knowing that we are not going to give up until we find out exactly what is happening. As for the medication? It is to help Daniel relax and is extremely mild."

Both parents looked at each other, confusion and concern pasted on their faces.

"Well, is this going to get worse? I mean, what do we have to do to stop it happening?" Alan asked, turning back to the unhelpful man sitting across from him.

"What we must do for now is keep monitoring him to identify exactly what is causing the seizures."

Alan wanted to leap from the chair and shout, *will you just do your fucking job and help my son get better*, but biting his tongue, he focused on the ceiling with scrunched eyebrows and shook his head. There was no doubt in anyone's mind just how angry he was.

"Right. I suppose we'll just go home and wait for him to grow out of it eh?" he said moments later.

Before the doctor had time to open his mouth, Alan and Rebecca were already on their way towards the door. Of course, he understood the man's frustration, but what he didn't want to admit to the couple was that he had never experienced or heard of anything like this with a patient before. They had a perfectly healthy son, and even with various other consultant examinations, they still hadn't found an answer to why the young boy experienced the fits.

Later that evening, as the thick darkness crawled its way over the countryside, the family sat at the kitchen table eating one of Alan's favourite's: chips, coleslaw, and lasagne.

Looking towards his son, Alan made a funny face at him as Daniel raised the food to his mouth. Daniel spurted a welcome laughter around the room, which caused both parents to smile with happiness.

What's going on in that little head? Alan wondered as those innocent blue eyes stared back at him.

"Okay, enough now. Eat your dinner," Rebecca said to the boy.

Turning to her, she then folded her bottom lip outwards to form part of a funny face, causing the boy to giggle uncontrollably.

While she switched off his bedroom light later that evening, Rebecca stared at her son wrestling with his eyes as he drifted off to sleep, hoping that she and Alan would have answers soon.

The clock on the dressing table struck 3:13am as Alan slowly prised his weary eyes open. The moonlight illuminated the window curtains, gouging its way through the darkness within the room.

Lovely. Another few hours in bed, he said to himself, looking towards the red digits in front of him. He then straightened his legs and curled his toes as he enjoyed a pleasant stretch followed by a long yawn. Turning around on the mattress, he placed his arm over Rebecca, who faced away from him.

Just before he nodded off to sleep, he twitched and inhaled quickly.

What causes that? He smiled to himself, cuddling into his girlfriend farther. His eyelids became heavy once more as he listened to her breathing softly beside him.

It was then a slight unexplainable uncomfortableness creeped over him; a feeling that something else was in the room. He peered above Rebecca's right shoulder into the dimness and saw nothing out of the ordinary.

Cop on will you! He scolded himself. *There's nothing in the room, you idiot.*

But the more he thought about it, something about the quiet stillness of the room just didn't feel right to him.

He turned and raised himself onto his elbows, an instant, sharp shiver ran the length of his spine. At the foot of the bed lurked a small, dark figure. He froze with fear, not knowing how to react.

"What are you doing?" Rebecca asked, groggily.

He didn't reply, just gazed at the motionless shadow in front of him. Another deep inhale broke the unsettling silence.

"Alan?" Rebecca asked, turning to see what he stared at.

He placed a hand on hers to help reassure her as best as possible, and then he slowly reached for the bedside light. Rebecca almost broke his hand, awaiting whatever it was staring at them to lunge for their necks.

Flicking on the switch, both were shocked to find their son standing at the end of the bed, gazing blankly at them.

"Daniel?" Rebecca called.

No response.

"Daniel?" she called again with a more authoritative tone.

No response. Not even a single blink of an eye.

Alan climbed from the bed, and slowly approached his son.

"He must be sleep walking," he whispered.

"You're not meant to wake anyone while they're sleep walking," Rebecca said, unable to hide the worry in her voice.

"I'm not going to."

Alan examined Daniel and waved a hand in front of his eyes, which warranted no reaction whatsoever. He then went over and switched on the bedroom light. Daniel giggled in a low tone.

Alan returned to him, placed a hand on his shoulder, and asked, "Daniel, are you okay?"

The child laughed loudly, still staring straight

ahead.

"Daniel?" he asked once again as concern made its way into both parents' minds.

Then the laughter stopped, and the young boy stood with hefty eyelids, looking around the room. He stopped at his mother, she could tell he was extremely disorientated.

She climbed from the bed, surprised she hadn't wet the mattress, and went over to her son.

She checked his forehead for any signs of high temperature. His skin was icy cold.

"Come on, pet. Let's get you back to bed," she said softly, taking his hand and led him from the room.

"Are you okay? Do you remember anything?" she asked the child, tucking him into his bed.

"Just the scary man," he said.

"Don't worry. It was just a bad dream. Get some rest now, okay." She softly rubbed his head.

The child nodded. She kissed him on the cheek and then walked towards the door. She switched off the bedroom light, and as she pulled the door closed, she swore Daniel giggled. Peeking back into the darkness, nothing more was heard. She didn't bother going back in, and elected to let her son get some sleep instead of unnecessarily disturbing him.

"Is he okay?" Alan asked, sitting on the edge of the bed as Rebecca returned to their room.

"He is back in his bed. I think he had a nightmare, got scared, and didn't realise where he was."

"Well, he nearly gave me a heart attack." Alan grinned.

"You're not the only one. I didn't know who it was at the end of the bed," Rebecca added.

The pair then climbed back into the bed.

"I hope it has nothing to do with his illness," Rebecca said as Alan replaced his arm around her.

"I'd say it was just a nightmare like you said."

Eventually the pair drifted off to a peaceful slumber.

Chapter 19

Another month passed, and Daniel's fits became more frequent and violent. Without warning, he would collapse—much to the dismay of everyone around him—and shake around.

Saturday evening came, and two days had stretched by without any upsets. They had just finished eating dinner and had settled on the couch to watch some TV comprised mostly of gameshows.

Alan enjoyed the comfort of the evening and battled closing eyelids. As the clock struck 8:03, Daniel struck the floor.

Both parents leaped from the sofa to help their son. Alan quickly laid down on the floor on his stomach and cradled the child's head to prevent any serious injuries as he rattled around the floor. Rebecca kneeled beside him, in order to reassure him that everything was going to be okay.

"Nothing will ever be okay again!" the boy growled.

Both parents' eyes widened and jaws plummeted lower as concern marched across their faces.

"He'll never get rid of me." Slurred from the young boy's contorted mouth.

A vicious laughter projected from the boy, and just as quickly as the fit occurred, it ceased.

Both parents helped their son back onto the sofa and reassured him that the seizure was over and he was okay. Rebecca fetched him some water to sip, and for the remainder of the evening, kept both eyes on him.

"That's the first time he's ever done that," Rebecca said as she climbed into the bed, after checking on Daniel. She was still shaking from the events earlier that evening. "What was he talking about?"

"We will contact the hospital first thing Monday morning and try and get some bloody answers once and for all! There is no point calling now because none of Daniel's doctors work over the weekend," Alan replied.

"Okay, but we can't let this keep going. He just seems to be getting worse and worse."

"I know. Don't worry. We'll get to the bottom of this. Now, try to get some sleep, okay?" Alan said, leaning across and kissing her on the forehead.

Alan's eyelids unwrapped at 3:23am. He looked at the blurred digits in front of him, wiped his eyes, and then recognised how early it was.

Before he could relish the amount of hours to enjoy before he had to actually climb from the blankets, his head twitched to attention upon hearing a creak outside the bedroom door left open.

He listened attentively, and moments later, another creak crept into the room from the concealed hallway. He swung his legs from the bed and approached the partially closed door. Alan didn't bother waking Rebecca as he didn't see any point in doing so. *Every house creaks during the night.*

Slowly pulling the door open—more so to prevent awaking Rebecca from her slumber—he inspected the darkness. At first, he kicked himself for giving into his curiosity. However, that was short-lived due to his heart skipping a beat as he witnessed something move within the dimness.

Whatever it was, it slowly moved towards the stairs. Alan's eyes adjusted to the night some more, and he then recognised the multi-coloured pyjamas.

"Daniel," he whispered, stepping into the hall.

No reply came.

"Daniel, what are you doing out of your bed at this hour?" he continued.

The young boy laughed, as he slowly made his descent downstairs.

Alan turned back towards his bed, where Rebecca still slept quietly. Deciding not to turn on the light upstairs in case Rebecca awoke worrying, he followed his son down to the kitchen.

Flicking on the light, he squinted through tired eyes and spotted Daniel glaring at his own reflection in the large window pane within the back door. Approaching him, he could hear the boy inhaling slowly and deeply.

"Are you okay Daniel?" he asked, moving around the kitchen table towards the child.

Alan looked beyond the boy's shoulders at the

reflection on the glass, sweat streamed down his son's face. But what disturbed him more was the eerie grin on the child's face as he stared at his father behind him.

He felt the dampness through the fabric, as he placed his hand on the child's shoulder.

"He is inside," slowly fell from Daniel's mouth.

"Who?" asked Alan, assuming he was having another bad dream.

"He's inside. He's inside. He's inside," the child shouted frantically.

Rebecca shot from the bed and fumbled her way down to the kitchen, where she found Alan hugging the distraught boy.

"What happened?" she asked, rubbing her son's forehead.

"I followed him down here. He's okay. I think he just had a nightmare. I'll take him back up in a second," Alan replied, not wanting to worry Rebecca.

After tucking him back into bed, Alan entered the bedroom where he was greeted by Rebecca sitting upright on the mattress.

"He didn't have another seizure, did he?" she asked, worry flooding her eyes.

"No, pet, he didn't. It was just a dream."

"What was he shouting? Is he getting worse?" she asked.

"Don't worry. We will call the hospital on Monday and get him more help."

The heaviness of Rebecca's eyes was soothed by

their closure soon afterwards.

However, lying in the darkness, Alan never closed his eyes. He lay pondering what Daniel meant when he repeated, *he's inside,* and why was he smiling at him moments before.

Chapter 20

Six months crawled by, and Daniel's health had deteriorated to the point he stopped eating. Alan and Rebecca were still no closer to an answer to what was happening to the boy.

Both parents were mentally destroyed. Their son had an illness with no name, no cause, and no cure.

"Let me get that for you," Rebecca said, as she fought back the tears, lacing up Daniel's runner.

She turned to Alan, and his eyes were just as moist. He had set the table for himself and Rebecca and on one side stood a lonely glass and straw.

The frail boy's mother guided him over to the seat at the kitchen table then lifted him into the chair as a knife darted into her heart, watching his face grimace in pain. Alongside of not eating, numerous oozing sores and dark bruises had built up on his body. The doctors mainly put it down to inactivity and lack of nourishment. Daniel had been prescribed a cream to help ease the sores, but they appeared to only get worse.

"Let's get some dinner," Alan said, trying to brighten the atmosphere in the room as best he could.

He lay his and Rebecca's plates which contained potatoes, mixed vegetables, pork chops, and gravy on one side of the table facing Daniel's chair.

A loud humming sound bounced off the bright cream kitchen walls. Moments later, Alan poured a blended concoction of fruit and medicine into the glass in front of the young boy.

"How are you doing son?" Alan asked, in an effort to keep a positive attitude at the table; more so to encourage his son to try and eat something.

There was no reply. He just stared at the table through eyes which had nearly fallen back into his skull.

Both adults turned to each other wide-eyed with concern. Alan then placed a sliver of meat into his mouth, he hoped it would trigger a mirrored reaction from his son, but nothing.

"Are you going to try your drink?" Rebecca asked. "Here, let me help you."
She stood from her seat, lifting the glass to the boy's chapped mouth.

After swallowing a tiny sip, the boy coughed the liquid back up. Wiping his mouth, Rebecca sat back down. It had been common over the last number of weeks to keep very little food into his stomach. At first, the pair were frustrated, but all they could do was hope that he could somehow keep some of the food down.

Alan awoke later that night to the sound of his son screaming through the darkness. He leaped from the bed, followed closely by Rebecca, and almost smashed through the boy's bedroom door. He didn't even turn on the bedroom light.

"What's wrong, son?" he asked, assuming it was either a nightmare or the sores.

"He's in the room," the boy returned, as sweat seeped from his forehead.

"Don't worry, pet. There is no one here. It was just a dream," his mother said as she wiped his brow.

Alan couldn't help but glance around the room to check if there was someone lurking within the shadows. Nothing lunged at them.

"We're here now, okay? There is nothing to worry about," he said, turning back to his son.

"No, he's in here," the feeble boy said.

"Who?" asked Rebecca.

Meanwhile, Alan slowly peered around the room once more. *It can't be HIM,* he thought, as cold prickles danced their way up his back and across his shoulders. He then quickly stood from the bed, and flicked on the bedroom light.

"The man who lives in the dark. He is always here." Daniel wheezed out his words.

Both parents gazed at each other in shock; Alan more so as he thought about a particular night so many years ago, and the words that were uttered to him made him shit himself. *See you soon.* The words echoed in his head as though they were just spoken the day before, and the sinister smile projected across the road towards him was still etched in his mind after his parent's vicious murders. His mind had painfully wrestled with itself over the years trying to establish how the wicked figure could just disappear in front of him.

Struggling to brush the thoughts aside, he returned to Daniel's bedside.

"We'll make sure you're safe," Rebecca said.

Alan smiled as best he could across the mattress to show unity. He didn't want to worry Rebecca or his son any further than they already were.

An hour passed, and the boy had been asleep for twenty minutes. The couple decided to retire to their bed for the reminder of the night. They left both doors ajar in case Daniel had another nightmare.

Switching off their bedroom light, Daniel's eyes flicked open.

"Daniel," slowly crawled its way around the darkened room, spoken in a low, malevolent voice.

Before he covered his head with the blanket, he spotted the huge twisted figure making its way towards him from the corner of the room. Then darkness.

The following morning, Rebecca pried her exhausted eyes open and then quickly made her way to Daniel's bedroom. Pushing past the door, a putrid stench flowed into her nostrils. Pulling back curtains, the daylight outside seemed to have no effect on the darkness loitering within the bedroom.

"Come on, Daniel. Time for some breakfast, and then we're going to visit your doctor."

The boy didn't answer as she left the room to use the bathroom. Flushing the toilet moments later, she returned to the bedroom, glancing into her room as

Alan got dressed.

"Daniel, come now. Time to get up," she said, assuming he had pulled the blanket over his face in protest.

She reached for the cold blanket and dragged it from his face, slightly surprised not witnessing any movement beneath it. She inhaled sharply as she viewed her son's motionless, wide-eyed terror-filled, pale face.

"Daniel?" she roared, shaking him in the bed.

Seconds later Alan was beside her, "What's wrong?"

He lifted the boy from the bed and the child screamed, as if in agony.

"He's mine, and so are you!" Daniel growled in a deep tone, while squirming violently in his father's arms. "You've no fucking idea how sick you make me."

Daniel then stared at his father dead in the eye, grinned at him, and then he became limp.

"Daniel?" Alan roared, setting him down on the bed.

The boy's arms fell beside his lifeless body.

"DANIEL!" Alan shouted once more trying to shake him to life.

He turned to Rebecca who had already retrieved her mobile phone and was waiting for the emergency services to answer the call. Following flustered clutters of words, broken sentences, the operator on the other line was able to establish the address. She then instructed the pair to begin compressions on the child's chest to help keep the blood flowing around his paling body and informed Rebecca that an ambulance was on its way.

Alan tried to maintain any sliver of life within his son, as Rebecca exploded into tears.

"We can't lose him," she said.

Meanwhile, beads of sweat stung their way into Alan's eyes. He didn't stop to wipe them. His son was more important right now.

Eternity passed as Daniel's lifeless head continued to flap around on the bed, eyes dead, pointing towards the ceiling. The approaching sirens wailing through the fresh country air brought no relief to the couple. Pulling into the driveway, Rebecca had the door swung wide waiting for the paramedics to enter.

Pointing them upstairs to the bedroom, the paramedics pushed past the boy's frantic father and began working on him. All hope was lost after twenty minutes of relentless work to try save the boy's life, and he was pronounced dead.

The loud ambulance sirens were nothing compared to the cries of anguish and pain from the parents. Cradling Rebecca in his arms, Alan stared at his son's body, wondering what happened, and he hoped he would open his eyes from the nightmare, and find himself laying his bed at any moment.

"I'm sorry," the older, male paramedic said, which brought home the reality of the situation as they left the room to give the parents some time alone with their son.

"He was our little angel," Rebecca said rubbing the boy's brow.

A horrid laughter pushed its way into Alan's mind. He frowned, wondering where jeering came from and why, at such a moment, he would experience it. The laughter ceased, and moments later, he could have sworn that the words, *'see you soon,'* whispered their way around the room. However, the pain and loss searing through his body, alongside trying to console Rebecca, took priority.

"What are we going to do without him?" Rebecca asked taking her son's cold hand in her own.

Alan was unable to find words to form a reply. Instead, he held his girlfriend's free hand and swallowed hard. Standing, looking at his dead son, he felt a combination of emptiness and an internal, blunt, dense pain unlike anything he had experienced since his parents were murdered. Just as the grief was about to overpower him, a slight knock came to the bedroom door. The time had come to remove the body to establish the cause of death.

He's fucking dead. Can't you leave him in peace!
The paramedics placed the corpse onto the stretcher, which looked huge compared to the tiny body. Alan bit his tongue and allowed them to do their job out of respect for Rebecca who was still in emotional fragments on the bed.

Both parents were permitted to travel—not that

Alan would have been prevented from being with his son—in the back of the ambulance with Daniel to the hospital.

Daniel's doctor met them at the large glass doors.

"This is all your fucking fault. We told you something was wrong with him and you just couldn't do your fucking job, just test, test, test and no fucking answers!" Alan said through gritted teeth, clinching his fists, fighting every urge in his body to punch him in the face.

"I'm really sorry for your loss."

Rebecca paid no attention to the confrontation and followed the paramedics into the busy hospital.

Following an extensive examination, the results showed that the boy died from heart failure. That made absolutely no sense to the boy's parents, because most of the tests while he was alive had not one thing to do with his heart. As far as they knew, his heart was fine.

The funeral was celebrated the following Tuesday morning in the local church. Sitting in the mourning car as it steered through the gates, Alan stared at the stained glass doors trying to comprehend why his son was going to be carried through them in a coffin before him himself. The roars of a heartbroken mother bounced off the old stone walls throughout the ceremony, as Alan tried to console her as much as possible. They were surrounded by close family and friends, most of which were Rebecca's.

The smell of the incense and sight of the smoke plumes cast Alan into a daydream.

He remembered fondly playing football in the backyard with his son when he was healthy; of course, always letting him win. He remembered how it use to always bring a smile to his face listening to his boy laugh with joy.

All of that was gone and he would never get the horrid memories of his son's dying moments out of his mind.

"*Amen*" brought him back to reality as the final prayer was concluded beside the tiny open hole on top of Alan parent's grave, where the young boy was going to be laid to rest with his grandparents. Fr. Roche then invited the parents to sprinkle some clay on the small coffin as it was lowered into the welcoming ground, ready to consume the wooden box.

As she stood over the grave, Rebecca howled her son's name. Her pain could be heard far beyond the cemetery walls.

The pair then stood back as the gravedigger picked up a shovel—which had no doubt covered many people in its time—and began to sprinkle the soil onto and around the box, trying his best not to make eye contact with the devastated parents.

Mixed emotion flooded Alan's mind. He wanted to run over to the man burying his son, push him aside, and dig the boy back up and hold him once more, and he envisioned how life would be without his boy, and how would he ever be able to sooth Rebecca's hurt.

Breathing deeply, he glanced towards the people close by, and spotted some familiar faces.

Showing their support were his childhood friends Stephen, Anthony, and Christina.

"Thanks for coming guys," he said, following the final person shaking his hand and saying how sorry they were for his loss.

"The minute I heard, I got the first plane over. I'm so sorry, Alan. I've no idea how you must be feeling right now," Christina said, settling a warm hand on his right elbow.

"If there is anything we can do, let us know okay," Stephen added.

Alan nodded in reply and said, "I'm devastated. I don't know what I'm going to do without my boy, and I'm worried about how Rebecca is taking this. She hasn't spoken about Daniel since it happened." He attempted to wipe the tears building in his eyes.

The three friends surrounded Alan in a cocoon of hugs. The group then approached Rebecca, who stood, shattered beside the grave, and offered their condolences.

Following all the visits, Mass cards and phone calls, the house slowly slipped into an unusual quietness. Life smashed the couple in the face. Gone was the playful laughter which use to hop off the walls within the house. Gone was the family atmosphere. Gone was their only child. Gone was the life which would never be the same again.

Chapter 21

"It's a lovely day out there. Wanna go for a walk or something later?" Alan asked, stepping into the bedroom, glancing towards the curtains as they shielded the window. The sunlight outside tried its best to poke through.

"No, I'm fine here." Rebecca spat from beneath the blankets, followed by a quick shuffle and deep sigh.

A little over two months had passed since Daniel was lowered into the ground, and Rebecca had rapidly plunged deep into a morbid pit. She no longer wanted to have social interaction and spent most of her time in bed. The only time she ventured from her seclusion was to use the bathroom or snack on junk food.

"Are you sure?" Alan sat on the mattress beside her.

Pulling back the duvet, he eyed her pale expression and weary eyes. *What is she doing to herself?* He thought, resting a hand on her shoulder

"Yeah, I'll be fine. You go."

Scrunching his eyebrows, frustration wove its way into his mind. He wanted to grab and shake her and roar *he was my son too*, but he declined, leaving her in peace, coming to the conclusion that this may drive her further into her desolate shell.

As he stepped out into the blissful winter sunshine, Alan took in a deep breath. *Maybe I should stay in the bed as well.* But he knew that was no way to mourn his child's death. Setting up along the road with the chirps of birds and the slight whooshing of traffic on the main road in the distance, he could still see Daniel playing on the road, which seemed like forty years ago to him. Passing the homes of his childhood friends, he felt like a stranger. Most of the neighbour's faces were unrecognisable to him. Most of his memories here consisted of pain, torment, and loss with a sprinkle of happiness thrown in every so often.

Nearing the end of the road, he took in the old, dilapidated Moore's house. A slight unease came over him, eying the moss-covered roof, crumbling walls, falling door, and smashed windows. He recalled how much the residents of the building scared him and how they were wrongly accused of kidnaping and hurting him. He still hated himself for being such a coward. *Maybe if I had of just went straight home that evening instead of hiding, Frank would be still alive!* Had constantly haunted him over the years, alongside the thoughts of his parent's cruel deaths.

Alan quickly turned on his heels upon hearing a piercing scream. Moments later, a second scream ran its way up the road towards him. *Rebecca!*
He panicked, and ran as fast as possible towards the house. Unlocking the door, he raced upstairs, burst through the bedroom door, and saw Rebecca, fear

engraved onto her face, sitting upright on the bed.

"What's wrong?" he asked, catching his breath, forehead slightly moist.

She sat wide-eyed, trembling beneath the blankets.

"Rebecca?" he asked, walking towards her.

"Someone was here," she said.

"What? In the house?" Alan asked with scrunched eyebrows, looking around quickly, with his fist clinched.

"No point looking for him. He's gone."

"Who?" he asked.

"I don't know, but he said he has Daniel and always will. He said we are his too before disappearing." She collapsed into a deluge of tears.

Alan shuttered as a chill crossed through him then joined her on the bed.

"I'm sure it was just a dream. You need to get out of this room."

"I know what I saw and heard," she spat back at him.

"What did you see?" he asked, hoping not to start a fight.

"I couldn't see him properly, but there was a dark figure standing in the corner, speaking in my father's voice. I knew it wasn't him. He wanted me to get up and take his hand. When I refused, he began to mock me about having Daniel, and he said he would be back soon for us."

As cold tears pattered against his t-shirt, he

remembered the promise made to him by the demon so many years ago. He pondered if this was all just a coincidence. Was there someone in the room? Was Rebecca just dreaming and hadn't fully snapped out of it when she spoke to this *man*? Or was there something else going on?

His primary concern at that moment was to ensure Rebecca was safe and try to comfort her as much as possible, and then try to piece together what was going on.

As a thick darkness swept across the land that night, Alan ensured all the doors and windows were locked before he joined Rebecca in the bedroom. Looking at her lying somewhat peacefully asleep, he wished he could turn back time to when they were all a little, happy family. However, those days no longer existed, and they would have to try their utmost to continue on without their beloved son.

The rain patted off the window as Rebecca awoke in the early hours of the morning, aided by some partial moonlight breaking through the cloud cover, she glanced at the window, taking in the trickles of water flowing down the glass. She turned and became comfortable once more. Before closing her eyes, she uncontrollably twitched on the mattress. She turned again in order to obtain some form of rest. However, she was abruptly startled by the sound of a child's laughter.

Holding her breath, she bolted upright in the bed, and looked towards the open door. About twenty seconds passed, and nothing. Then she spotted a small figure run past the door, followed by some playful giggles.

Daniel, she thought, leaping from the bed and running towards her son. She didn't think to wake Alan due to her eagerness to hold her child once more.

Following the boy downstairs, she witnessed him opening the front door and stepping outside into the dark, damp night. Without a second thought she pursued him.

"Daniel?" she called, stepping closer to the small shadow standing at the gate in front of the house. "Is that you?"

"Can I have a hug, Mammy?" the concealed figure asked.

She attempted to dry the rain from her face and eyes to view the boy better.

"Of course. Come on in out of the rain."

There was no reply, just an emotionless shadow looking back at her.

"Daniel, come in out of the rain." She instructed once more.

The boy stretched out a hand for his mother to aid him back inside. Then it struck her. *My son's dead,* she reconfirmed to herself as the brutal reality of the event hit home.

"You're not Daniel, are you?" she muttered, as the rain stabbed her eyes.

A sadistic laughter howled from the darkness.

Rebecca took a cautious step backwards, and the *child* took a step forward, the moonlight revealed the pale boy's face and large white eyes.

"Your soul smells delicious. I'll enjoy ripping it apart!" he said.

She shrieked in terror, waking Alan in the process.

He lay there, disorientated for a moment, wondering if he was dreaming, but the empty space beside him quickly proved otherwise. A second scream burst through the house. He leaped from the bed and ran downstairs, out the front door, and joined Rebecca. Meanwhile, the demonic figure had disappeared.

"What are you doing out here?" he asked, ignoring the chilling, excruciating cold making its way up through his feet from the sapping ground.

"I thought it was Daniel, but it wasn't him." She shivered beside him.

"What do you mean?"

"I followed something out here. It told me it was going to enjoy ripping my soul apart," she said as she quickly glanced around the darkness, terrified that they may be attacked at any moment.

Alan's eyes widened and his jaw almost hit the damp ground beneath him.

"Come on, let's get back inside." Composing himself, he placed his arm around her saturated pyjamas and guided her back towards the door.

After they changed from their wet clothes, Rebecca sat at the kitchen table. Alan made her a warm cup of tea with plenty of sugar to help with the shock.

"You thought it was Daniel?" he asked sitting across from her, as his concern grew.

"In the beginning, I did, but whatever it was, it was pure evil. What's happening to us? First our son, and now this?" She cried into the palms of her trembling hands.

"Your mind is overworked. You need some proper rest, and to get out of that room during the day. It's driving you crazy hiding away up there." He said trying to reassure Rebecca.

Maybe he's right, trickled through her mind. *Maybe I am just hearing and seeing things. That would explain a lot.*

Nodding in agreement, she took a sip of tea from the cup and then followed him up to bed.

Chapter 22

Another month had dragged by, and Rebecca had delved further into her dark infested abyss. She suffered constant nightmares and *visitations* from an evil only witnessed by the deteriorating woman.

Rebecca had practically given up eating altogether. She hadn't washed herself in weeks, and she had begun whispering, occasionally shouting at the invisible fiend.

It was an overcast Saturday afternoon. Alan had just gotten off the phone with Rebecca's mother who had called to see how things were. Of course, he didn't tell her the full story, as he prayed that Rebecca would snap out of it so he wouldn't have to needlessly worry the elderly woman.

I'm slowly losing everything. He thought. Obviously, he was heartbroken and missed Daniel more each passing second, but he also wanted to respect his son's memory and try in some way to move on. However he could feel his grip loosening on Rebecca and whatever life they had left together.

Over the week or so, Rebecca said a man use to come to visit her every night at exactly 3am. She said he didn't wake her. She literally would twitch from her sleep and he would be at the end of the bed, whispering to her. At first, he claimed to be sent from God, there to help, and wanted to bring her to see her son one more time. While he sat on the sofa, Alan remembered the fear engraved on her face as she told him that the visitor would extend a hand and say *all you have to do is reach out and I'll take you to see him one last time.*

Things became aggressive once she kept refusing. He began saying that Daniel will never be at rest, there are worse places than the hell humans can imagine, and that he would show her soon. He said that humanity makes him sick, and that he enjoys showing everyone there is something to be scared of after death.

Alan had quizzed what he looked like on many occasions, however Rebecca said he never revealed himself; he always remained in the shadows, tempting her to join him.

All the torment built up within Alan like a pressure release valve, ready to pop at any second. He felt useless and couldn't understand why Rebecca was being plagued by this evil and wondered if it was all just in her head..

Alan dragged himself from his slumber to the sound of Rebecca sobbing beside him.

"Go away!" she roared into the forbidden darkness.

Alan sat up, his eyes struggled to adjust to the blackness within the room.

"What are you doing?" he asked.

"He's here," she said, trembling in the bed beside him causing the mattress to quiver.

Alan rubbed his eyes to focus his vision and glared around the room, he found nothing looming at them. He stood from the bed and approached the light switch as Rebecca winced behind the blanket. Turning on the dazzling light, he found the room as empty just like moments before.

"You need to help me Alan, I don't know who or why he is doing this." She cried out.

He quickly returned to her and comforted her until she surrendered to tiredness.

Lingering on this thought, the following morning after some breakfast, he decided to go upstairs to check if she was okay, after all he did love her and he just wanted her suffering to end. Ascending the stairs he heard rummaging from the bedroom.

Quickly opening the door, he stepped inside to find Rebecca on her hands and knees frantically scrubbing the carpet in the corner of the room. Beside her stood a pink, plastic bucket and most of the water and disinfectant it had contained was now seeping into the fabric it sat on. Her hands were a glaring white and deep wrinkles and cracks had already began to cover her palms and back of her hands like some elaborate road map.

"What are you doing?" burst form his shocked mouth.

"I'm trying to wash him away, maybe if I clean where he usually stands, he won't come back." She

155

tried to explain her motive and continued to wildly scrub the dulled material.

He walked over to her, the squishing sound of the carpet filling his ears, and held her arm.

"You don't need to do this. No one is after you." He announced in an effort to calm her down.

"There fucking is!" she screamed, turning and smacking him on the head with the wooden scrubbing brush she had nearly worn to a nub.

Alan stood back from her amazed, as the blood began to dribble from the open wound above his right eye. She emotionlessly turned from him and continued with her work. It was clear to him that she wouldn't stop until she was satisfied. It was also clear to him now that the fine line between sanity and madness was being stretched to its limits and he didn't know how much pressure the fragile string would take before it finally snapped. Stepping back down stairs, holding the surprisingly stinging wound, he wondered what to do to help break the ever growing wedge between himself and the woman he still truly loved.

Steeping a small cloth under the cold tap, he applied it to the cut above his eyebrow. He considered ringing Rebecca's parents, but he quickly forced the thought from his mind, questioning *what kind of man am I, going to ring her parents for help?*

Dabbing the wound for a brief moment the blood loss began to ease, as did the anger he felt towards his girlfriend.

For the rest of the evening he remained downstairs, mostly contemplating whether or not to seek help. Before going to bed he decided to give her a few more days, he would talk to her tomorrow and if she did not come to her senses soon he would seek professional help to try to regain the Rebecca of old once more.

Before Alan flicked off the bedroom light he viewed the damp, faded spot in the corner, and then eyed Rebecca curled up in the bed, obviously tired from her days work. He was tempted to run to the bed, hug her and say that he would rid her of her tormenter once and for all, but the tense atmosphere between the pair still lingered in the air. He also contemplated whether or not her mind was being crushed by the grief of losing their son. Alan had no answers.

Alan awoke from his slumber in the early hours of the following morning and instantly noticed an empty bed beside him. He sat up assuming to be met by the light from the bathroom slicing through the heavy darkness, but nothing. Pulling the blankets off himself he could hear the rain slapping against the window outside.

"Rebecca?" he called.

The only answer was the environmental Morse code sounding against the glass.

"Fuck sake!" he said stepping into the damp patch on the floor in his bare feet as he made his way to the top of the stairs.

157

Flicking on the landing light, he was still none the wiser to the whereabouts of Rebecca. Reaching downstairs he checked the front door handle, locked. He made his way into the kitchen,

"Rebecca, where are you?" he asked as he turned on the kitchen light to reveal nothing at all. The rain continued to beat off the walls and roof outside,

Suddenly his attention turned to the *slapping* noise outside, like the sound of bare feet pacing back and forth on wet concrete. He stepped over to the curtain and peeked out into the darkness, his vision slightly obstructed by his own reflection. He leaped back from the glass as something quickly passed in front of him outside. Adrenaline rapidly began to pulsate through him. He grabbed a knife from the kitchen drawer. Without any delay he unlocked the back front and marched out into the night. He was shocked to find Rebecca pacing back and forth, saturated from head to toe. Taking hold of her he glanced towards her blooded, blue feet.

"He's inside, he's inside, he's inside," she muttered through a rattling mouth. Instantly he thought of Daniels same claim which by now seemed years ago, before he died.

"Who?" he asked as he brought her inside.

"He's inside, he's inside," she slowly returned.

Tending to her wounds, he felt the bitter effect of the cold concrete from her feet. This was the final straw, she had broken him, he was stumped and now needed to seek help from someone who knew exactly what to do.

Settling Rebecca into the now cold bed, he switched off the light and threw his arm around her shivering body, hoping to reintroduce some heat to her body and comfort her, all at the same time. He wasn't going to let this continue any longer, tomorrow he was going to get her the help she needed and by now not a second too soon.

Awaking the following morning to the sound of birds singing, he briefly remained in bed, enjoyed the song before the events of the previous night flooded into his mind and quickly changed his mood.

"You okay love?" he asked sitting to the side of the bed, rubbing the tiredness from his face. *Love*, he thought, *I wonder if she still loves me.*

A few mumbles and a quick shuffle was the response.

He decided to get dressed and leave her be. Not bothering with any breakfast; he set off towards the health clinic in town, he wanted to gain some closure on the last number of weeks once and for all.

As he walked along the country road with the wildlife whistling him along his way, fond memories flowed into his mind, which included the double smiles thrown at him when they played chase in the back garden as Rebecca grabbed Daniel, lifting him and shielding him from his father. His eyes wetted thinking about how he and Rebecca had spoken some time ago about trying for another child so Daniel would have a brother or sister to play with. That idea lay in the long, distant, happy past, and he wasn't sure if they would ever be in a position again to discuss anything even remotely associated with their future.

Sitting in the clinic waiting room, he was unable to fight the feeling of defeat creeping its way slowly through him. He had promised himself he would be strong and support Rebecca through the tragic time, but he was beaten and seeking help. He knew no shame should be felt sitting in the seat, waiting to be called into the room as everyone else gazed on, but he felt like he shouldn't be there. However, on the other hand, he had run out of options.

"Alan?" the elderly woman nodded to him with raised eyebrows.

He lifted himself from the seat and followed her into the room. She began with the usual questions: name, age, address, next of kin, and reason for the visit before he outlined that he was visiting on behalf of someone else. She then began all over again with the same dialogue and queried why Rebecca hadn't visited herself. He explained the situation, her current behaviour, and asked if she would call out to examine the rapidly deteriorating woman.

"Thanks, Dr. McKenna," he said eyeing her name badge, after agreeing to come out to examine Rebecca.

Pulling a jacket around her tiny frame, she locked the door behind her. She was a short lady, with short, curly, multi-coloured grey hair. Looking at her, Alan was amazed that the large glasses hadn't fallen to the ground as they barely balanced on the tip of her nose.

She offered to drive, which Alan gladly accepted, however he soon regretted taking her up on the offer as he would have walked faster back to the house.

"Rebecca, are you up?" he called, stepping in through the front door, followed closely by Dr. McKenna. The bedroom curtains had not been pulled back.

There was no response.

"She must be still in bed," he explained. "Take a seat and I'll go get her."

The doctor took her seat and Alan made his way upstairs. He pushed the door open to find the tossed bed empty. Then his attention was quickly drawn to the gloomy corner behind the door.

Alan took a quick, deep inhale as shock ricocheted around his body. On the floor lay Rebecca's limp body, her lips a darkened blue. Scattered beside her were a vast amount of various tablets, and scrapped on the wall beside her were the words, *I'm sorry. I couldn't take any more.*

"Rebecca," he roared as he tried to shake her back to life.

Her lifeless head arched away from him as he tried to sit her up, hoping her eyes would open, the only movement was the froth crawling from her mouth.

"Jesus, what have you done?" he asked aloud, the adrenaline kicking in, his mind unable to cope with the shock.

The door slapped him in the back, as the doctor made her way into the room.

"Quick help her!"

Her first reaction was to phone for help and then she began CPR, but judging by the coldness and colour of the body, it was already too late.

Alan stared on with a numbing ring filling his head. Looking at her head twitching on the floor, he knew her life had well and truly left her corpse. His eyes exploded into tears, realising that the one and only person left that meant the world to him had crossed over to the next one.

When the ambulance arrived, they pronounced her dead at the scene and removed her frail body to the hospital to establish the obvious cause of death.

Alan never left her side until he was politely asked to do so to carry out the examination, which concluded that she died as a result of ingesting a mixture of tablets.

With his already broken heart smashed into three million pieces, Alan would have to attend a loved one's funeral once more. Sitting in the lonely hospital waiting room, trying to rationalise what the fuck he had done to deserve such horrendous pain and suffering, a blanket of regret and guilt encased him. He wished he had told her once more just how much he loved her and he wished that he had sought professional help sooner.

Maybe then she would be still alive.

The next challenge would be to break the news to Rebecca's parents. The hospital staff had offered to help relieve him of the task, but he declined. He owed them that much at least.

Chapter 23

Dressing himself on the morning of Rebecca's funeral, Alan felt as dead as her. He no longer wanted to climb out of bed or to talk to anyone, because they would surely bring up his stiff, dead, love.

After her funeral celebration, he stood beside the open grave and stared blankly upon the coffin holding her dead remains. He tried to rationalise the events over the last number of weeks, but no amount of words on Earth could explain the pain. His son was gone. His girlfriend was gone. His life was gone.

Thinking back, he blamed himself. *Maybe if I just got her help sooner, rather than just sitting there thinking about my pride, she would be still alive.*

He tortured himself relentlessly. He appreciated the huge impact the loss of their son had on Rebecca, but it should have never driven her to that. He hated himself, and he didn't know how he was going to get through another cruel loss in his life.

Swallowing the huge lump in his throat, he wiped his moist eyes with the back of his hand. *How helpless must she have felt? What kind of man am I when the very person I loved couldn't confide in me?*

"I'll never forgive myself for letting things come to this, Rebecca. I'm so sorry. I hope you're finally at peace," he said before he turned and began his journey home.

Images of her pain flooded his mind, from her declaring that something evil was constantly plaguing her to the night he found her pacing back and forth in the back yard. He did consider the odd aspect, that he had to unlock the back door and she didn't have the key on her, but at that stage, her mind was so fragmented, he just assumed she climbed out a window or something. He would have checked if any windows were open, however, he was concerned more so on getting her back inside the house that night.

Following an evening of people telling him how sorry they were and if he needed anything let them know, he hugged Rebecca's parents goodbye. John drove but at a speed no faster than a snail's pace, so it'd be some time before they reached home. One comfort Alan noted was that they still had each other to confide in over their loss which no doubt only gets harder to deal with, and he had no one.

Pottering around the house that night, every single item brought back a memory of his dead girlfriend or son. Trying to keep his mind active proved impossible as every passing moment brought fourth more pain and loneliness. He decided to retire to bed early knowing there was no point staring blankly at the TV.

As he inched through the bedroom door, he shot his gaze towards the ground where he found Rebecca's paralysed, lifeless body. A wave of sadness and guilt crashed over him.

Should I even be in here so soon after her death? He fought against the mental struggle and reluctantly climbed into the frosty bed.

Alan lay staring at the ceiling for an eternity pondering the unchangeable past. *Maybe I should have ... What if I ... I wish I ...* where the beginnings of the numerous distressing sentences overwhelming his mind. He swung his attention to the empty mattress beside him and thought of the huge torment Rebecca must have suffered to force her to take her own life. Alan thought about joining her, but he questioned if he would have the guts to pull the trigger and end it all.

An overworked mind led to exhaustion, and eventually Alan's eyelids began to stitch themselves together. Just before he drifted off to sleep, he twitched to alertness. He shuffled around in the plentiful blankets and tried closing his eyes once more. The door slowly squeaked open.

He paid little attention, assuming it must be a draft passing through the house, causing the door's movement. Then the door slammed shut, causing him to leap upright in the bed. He stared at the door a long moment before a slow, deep, evil laughter slithered its way around the room.

"Who the fuck—" Alan uttered, as he clambered from the bed.

"I've been watching you for quite some time now, Alan. Humans are so easy to manipulate and break. I really enjoyed watching you suffer."

"Show yourself!" he ordered.

The laugher mocked him again.

He then eyed a huge silhouette within the shadows in the corner his girlfriend said her visitor would lurk. Alan lunged at the figure without a second thought, hitting only the solid wall.

"You couldn't protect your pathetic son or your rotting bitch from me, what makes you think you can protect yourself?" The voice came from the other side of the room.

Alan turned and was clawed across the chest, leaving four large gashes carved on it. He was then grabbed by the dark figure and slammed hard to the ground. Out of the darkness peered those two bright white eyes.

"I've taken everyone you've loved, and I'll enjoy taking you!" the demon said.

"That was you causing Daniel's fits, and you drove Rebecca to kill herself!" Alan said, realising that his son was never ill. Natas had possessed him and driven Rebecca insane.

A sharp-toothed smile came as the response. Natas pinned Alan against the wall and inserted four claws deep into his stomach. "Worthless!"

A mixture of gasps for air and splutters filled the room.

"Your pathetic soul belongs to me. I'll enjoy tearing it to pieces as you suffer over and over again."

Alan reached for the creature's hand, in a

pointless effort to prevent death. The beast closed its fist and tore away a huge chunk of flesh and muscle.

"There is no hope after death!" Natas said, basking in the suffering he inflected on the man.

Growing extremely cold, Alan knew death was close, he had failed his family, and gazed into the demonic eyes. Natas had waited all those years to attack Alan so he could inflect as much torment and pain as possible. Before he took his last breath, Alan cast his thoughts to his childhood friends, and judging by the grin on the demonic face in front of him, everyone else would soon experience the brutality of this evil fiend.

Alan went limp in the creature's hand as the majority of his blood drained onto the floor around him. Discarding him to the floor, the beast stood and looked down at Alan's body then left the remains there to fester and decay.

Chapter 24

Alan lay rotting on the bedroom floor one week before Fr. Roche decided to pop around to see how he was doing.

It was a glaring day. One which was a rare occurrence during the cold, bland winter months. After three raps on the front door, he turned to admire the peaceful country atmosphere. A minute passed, he knocked on the door once again, and listened for any movement inside. He lingered on the door step for another five minutes.

Assuming he was out, Fr. Roche turned to leave. Then something behind the frosted glass caught his eye. He couldn't be certain, but he was sure it looked like a huge, dark shadow standing there, staring back at him.

"Alan?" he called.

Nothing in reply.

"Alan, is that you?"

The only answer came as a slight stance shift, as if unnerving presence studied the priest. A shiver ran down his back, like he was being confronted in a stare down, as though the door didn't stand between him and the threatening figure.

"Where is Alan? I need to talk to him."

Whatever stared at him, didn't respond, just

slowly turned and disappeared into the darkness behind it.

Fr. Roche immediately pulled his phone from his pocket and dialled 999. After being instructed to stay outside, the Gardaí arrived soon afterwards. Fr. Roche quickly briefed them about what he saw and his concerns for Alan.

"Hello, Alan?" one Garda asked, banging aggressively on the door.

"Okay, stand back!" the other said, and kicked in the door.

"Stay behind us, okay." Both instructed the priest as they stepped into the unknown.

"Whoever it was, they were standing here," the priest confirmed, as he pointed to the floor beside the staircase.

"Alan, are you here?" an officer shouted once more, but his words fell onto the silent floors.

Finding absolutely nothing out of place, expect an overwhelming stink making them nauseous, they fought their way through it upstairs, the pong growing ever stronger. Staying alert, they slowly opened the first bedroom door, and found nothing unusual.

"Where is that smell coming from?" Fr. Roche asked, scrunching his eyebrows, curling his mouth downwards and briefly covering his nose.

As the Garda slowly pushed open the final bedroom door, he was met with a resistance. "There's something behind this."

The other Garda stepped in to give him a hand to force the door open. Instantly a swarm of flies whizzed around the dark room.

"Jesus!" the officer said, finding Alan's dead, partially rotted body.

Shocked, the priest stepped into the room, onto the dried blood, and began to pray over the blackening corpse. The two officers finished their search of the rest of the house, and couldn't locate the figure Fr. Roche claimed to have seen. They returned to witness the priest still praying over the dead, broken body.

"We're going to seal off the entire area for a forensic examination, Father. Please, don't touch anything and come outside once you're finished," the Gardaí instructed and respectfully left the room so the prayers could finish.

Once finished the prayers, Fr. Roche leaned down and drew the symbol of a cross on the dead man's forehead. Standing up, he stared at the body and wondered what may have caused the pain still engraved on the petrified face.

Three rapid, loud raps came to the bedroom door, causing his heart to skip beats.

"Just done," he said opening the door. Peering out into the hall, nobody could be seen.

A malevolent laughter sounded from behind him. He turned to find Alan standing, his head hanging to one side.

"Do you really believe in those insignificant words you just spoke?" the corpse said with a sinister smile, referring to the prayers spoken moments before.

"What are you?" he replied, as he tried his utmost not to show any form of fear, the door slowly creaked closed behind him.

The possessed body took a step forward.

"In the name of our Lord, I command you to stay where you are."

The decomposing face burst into a mocking laughter. "Tell me to stay where I am again!"

The priest reached into his jacket pocket and pulled out a small bible. He held the book out in front of him, closed his eyes, and begun to recite prayers.

Natas marched over and slapped the book out of the priest's hand.

"Words. That's all they are, is words," he growled.

"What are you?" the petrified man asked once more.

"I'll show you!"

The reanimated corpse placed both hands firmly on each side of its mouth and ripped the flesh apart. The rotting skin tore away from the bone between it like wet cardboard, eyes firmly fixed on the priest.

Fr. Roche stared on as vomit filled his throat.

Smiling, as the clumps of meat dangled from Alan's former jaw, Natas raised his hands and forced both thumbs into his eye sockets. Both eyes popped like water balloons followed by blood and other fluids flowing down the dead face from the dark red pits left behind.

"Jesus Christ!" the priest said, finally breaking his composure and tried unsuccessfully to open the door.

"You think he can help you? He has no power over me! I've existed long before he, or your so-called God."

"Look how fragile your bodies are?" Natas continued as he placed Alan's right hand onto his left arm.

He clawed and ripped the muscle from the arm. He took hold of a large chunk and threw it to the priest's feet.

The tattered body then lunged and grabbed the terrified man.

"Your turn," he spat. "I've plans for you!"

"What do you want?" the man roared, trapped against the wall.

"I want to torture every single soul on this Earth, I want to feel their suffering as I show them that once you die, you're all mine, and it all begins with you!"

He pressed on the priest's chest with his left hand.

"First, I'm going to snap your ribs then I'll tear your heart from your body, while you die wondering what torment awaits you when the darkness comes. But if you take my hand, it won't come to that," Natas said holding out Alan's right hand waiting for the priest to take it.

"I'll never take your hand!" he said with a strained voice.

Natas increased the pressure, the man's chest compressed farther, causing the ribs beneath it to click and crunch. Fr. Roche yelped.

"Just take my hand, and this will all end!" the demon said.

"Never!"

The demonic fiend applied more pressure, causing his lungs to flatten and breathing to cease. Staring into the smiling, possessed body's face, Fr. Roche panicked as *'what really is waiting for me after I die'* flew through his mind. His survival instinct kicked in, and he stretched out his hand in an effort to eliminate the excruciating pain.

Natas snatched it, and then nothing. The demon was gone, the body had returned to its original position, intact. The only injury evident was the one that put it on the floor in the first place.

The stunned man stood free from pain, as beads of sweat abseiled down his forehead, trying to establish what he had just been through. The door burst open, and in ran the two Gardaí.

"Is everything alright? We heard shouting," one asked as the other glanced around the room.

Slightly dizzy, Fr. Roche stepped away from the wall he had been pinned against moments before. "Everything is fine. I've finished praying." Was the only logical explanation that he could think of.

"Okay, come outside with us now."

He did as instructed, and joined the Gardaí outside while they waited for the forensic team to arrive.

After a full examination of the house and around the surrounding area, not one piece of evidence was unearthed. The body was finally moved to the hospital later that evening to carry out the post-mortem. The massive stomach injury was the obvious cause of death, but what couldn't be established was what inflected the wound. No finger prints were found on the huge, torn wound, and a lot of force would have had to have been used to cause such an injury.

They searched underneath Alan's fingernails for any skin or hair but again found nothing. Blood tests came back negative for intoxicants, and there were no other identifiable injuries on Alan's body. In a sense, it was like his stomach exploded from the inside out.

After gathering the post-mortem report, the Gardaí launched a murder investigation with little to go on.

Afterwards, Alan's broken torn body was released to very distant family, and of course, his childhood friends. Like before, in the same area, another murder lay unsolved.

Chapter 25

Three days after being released from the hospital, Alan's funeral was organised with Fr. Roche in the local church. However, the three days leading up to the day hadn't been sunshine and rainbows for the holy man.

The evening they discovered the corroded body, he couldn't get that demented, torn face out of his mind, and questioned whether the terrifying experience had happened at all.

You're stronger than this, he thought, reaching for one of the many books on the worn shelf beside the small, outdated television in the sitting room. He was a man of faith, and he was turning to some prayer for guidance. He opened the hardback cover and noticed that some pages had been ripped out. He turned his attention to the book shelf with no sign of them there.

"Only words," echoed around the room.

The startled man dropped the book, and shot his gaze around the room finding only his trembling shadow behind him. He walked to the sitting room door and peered into the dark splattered hallway. Nothing. He almost slammed his head off the door frame upon hearing a colossal crash behind him. Turning, he eyed the book support in pieces on the floor. He glanced left and right to uncover the cause but, as before, nothing seemed out of place.

He pulled back the blinds, and discovered that the window was closed. A draft scenario was out of the question.

Old fixings, he rationalised as he picked up the various religious literature.

"Only words!" slowly crawled their way around the room once more.

The priest darted upright, "Who's there?"

No reply came from the unsettling room, or the darkness trying to break in from the hallway.

Pull yourself together, Kevin, he told himself. *It's just in your head.* He assumed the horrific discovery in Alan's home was playing on his mind.

Finishing tidying the floor, he surrendered to the idea that he needed some rest to settle his tormented mind. He sat the final book on the coffee table, flicked off the light, and then made his way to the bedroom.

Resting his weary bones on the soft mattress, he cast his mental fishing line into his ocean of thoughts to reel in a comforting memory. However, the line kept getting snagged on the horrifying experience he wasn't sure he had suffered in Alan's room. After constant mental calculations about the apparent event he witnessed, he finally drifted off to sleep.

Awaking to a bright sunny morning, he stretched in the bed, which brought with it a pleasant feeling. Turning on the mattress, he heard fluttering within the blankets. Fr. Roche sat upright and spotted clumps of scrunched up paper at the foot of the bed. Reaching down and unravelling a page, he realised they were the missing pages from the book downstairs.

Unnerved, he climbed from the bed and gathered the rest of the paper flung around the room like confetti.

"What the—" he said, sieving through the torn pages, trying to rationalise what was going on.

His attention quickly turned to the mirror dangling on the wall. The pages fell to the floor as terror paralysed him. In the reflection, he eyed a huge, demonic figure staring back at him. He turned, and the monster was nowhere to be seen. As he turned his reluctant eyes back to the mirror, he witnessed a vomit-inducing scene. Standing there was the horned, slanted-mouthed creature—but more disturbingly— holding the priest's own decapitated head. The look of horror on the severed, blooded head was nothing compared to the expression on the shocked man's face. The beast smiled as those white eyes glared back at him through the glass. Natas flung the human trophy at the mirror, smashing the glass to pieces.

The priest leaped out of the way for fear of being smacked in the face by his own head. He expected to hear a thud followed by a rolling, rumbling noise as the head came to a halt against the far wall. But there was nothing.

Slowly climbing back to his feet, he peered into

the fractured mirror once more. The demon was gone. Joining his palms, he prayed.

He scrunched his eyebrows with frustration as unwelcome words flowed through his mind which included *worthless, fucking pitiful, only fucking words!* And most disturbingly were the words '*you're mine now!*'

Determined to not show weakness, he continued with his prayers. The voice in his head stopped, and he opened his eyes. He glanced towards his dark red hands, not realising just how hard he had clasped them together while banishing the unwelcome, resilient evil.

Recomposing himself, he exhaled and gathered the tattered pages. He pulled back the bedroom curtain to allow natural light into the shadow-filled room. After making his way from the room, he gripped the handrail firmly then slowly made his way down the stairs. A numbing ring squealed its way from ear to ear as he fought to keep his balance. Surviving the descent, he went outside to welcome some fresh air into his lungs.

He unlocked the front door and stepped into a bright, warm atmosphere. The disorientating humming gradually ceased as he inhaled the crisp country air. Taking in the scenery— which he usually enjoyed—he wondered what evil was at work, and if he had sent it packing its bags back to whatever dark pit the beast had crawled from.

He didn't have to query his question long, as the answer came when he turned to face his house.

Peering at one of the upstairs windows, he eyed someone lurking inside. He adjusted his position to obtain a better view, he quickly realised it looked exactly like the awestruck priest.

The creature behind the glass smirked at him, like before. Then it raised a hand and inserted the four fingers just below the jaw line. With ease it ripped the skin open. Blood splattered the window as the demon then proceeded to rip the skin completely off it's face, exposing the dark red, muscle-covered, skeletal face beneath. Unable to take any more demonic torture, the priest emptied his guts onto the ground beneath him.

Looking towards the window again, Natas was gone. There was no evidence to prove that it wasn't just the priest's imagination, except the previous horrific experience he had just been subjected to, until the words, "You belong to me," slithered their way to him along the slight breeze.

Fear encased his entire body as he locked the front door, deciding to stay away from the house and venture to church to pray further in an order to expel the evil once and for all.

After Mass and a full day of prayer, combined with some chit-chat with parishioners who visited the church to pray for their own specific reasons, he went home. Stepping into the dark evening—unlike that morning—the icy winter air patted his face as he made the walk home. Rounding the corner, he eyed his small, Irish cottage, but what stood out to him was the sitting room light as it beat its way through the thick night. Slowing his pace, his first thought was someone had broken in. He knew for a fact he had not left any lights on when he left the house that morning.

His heart thumped rapidly as he passed through the gate and snuck up to the naked window. Glancing through the glass, he saw no one inside. He moved towards the front door and discovered it still firmly secure. Puzzled, he eased the key into the lock, turned it, and remained on high alert in case someone darted past him with an armful of his belongings. However, he stepped into an empty house.

Noticing nothing missing, he made his way to the back door, and like the front, it was firmly locked shut. Moving around his home, he found no sign of any forced break in. As the priest pondered how the light had been left on, a loud crash boomed upstairs.

"Who's up there!" he roared, peering into the throbbing darkness concealing the top of the stairs, which seemed like it stretched on for miles into an abyss.

No reply, only silence filled his ears. He pressed the light switch, and it didn't work. Quickly glancing into the illuminated sitting room and then back towards the blackness, he began to make his ascent into the unknown. Every step he climbed, he prepared to turn and dart back out the door he had nervously stepped through moments before.

Reaching the landing, he once again tried the

light. To his relief, it worked. He went on to check his bedroom first. He didn't even need to flick on the bedroom light to realise exactly what had caused the smash. Scattered in pieces on the floor lay the mirror he had seen the demonic figure in earlier that day.

"Why are you doing this?" he said aloud, reaching into his pocket and taking out rosary beads.

The light downstairs popped, followed by the one just outside the room. Surrounded in complete darkness, a low, deep laughter floated around him.

"I told you, those words can't help you!" sounded in his mind.

Fr. Roche knew he was plagued by a powerful evil, and he decided the best way to fight it was to ignore it.

That worked until after the Mass he said over Alan's coffin in the church on the night prior to the funeral Mass to be held on the day of the man's burial. He awoke in his bed as an ear aching ringing drilled through his head. He cursed the darkness as he climbed from the bed to find the source of the paralysing sound. The sound intensified, causing him to place both palms on either side of his head to reduce its effectiveness. There was no change. Realising the noise came from within him, he dropped to his knees.

"Get out of my head!" he cried, his face expressing extreme agony. The mind-numbing sound increased, accompanied by laughter again, and finally, the priest couldn't take any more of the torture and passed out.

Visions of torture bombarded his shattered mind. He was in a dank dark room. In the distance, agonising screams came from all directions. The back of his right hand was placed against the palm of his left, above his head. Numerous nails had been beaten through both hands and bent around his wrists, holding him in place against the freezing wall. Coming to his senses, he moaned, arching his bare back from the wall.

Something then caught his eye amongst the churning darkness. He inhaled, sharply eyeing the demonic beast slowly approaching him.

"So fucking pathetic!" Natas snarled. "Have you any idea how easy this was?"

"Let me go now!" the priest said.

The slanted mouth opened, and out spouted an erratic laughter, which made the muscles in the priest's back tighten.

"Why are you doing this? What do you want?" the broken spirited man asked as the blood from his wounds flowed down his arms and splashed to the ground beneath him.

The fiend shot across the room and grabbed the priest by the neck.

"What do I want?" Natas roared. "I want to destroy every pitiful soul in your wretched fucking world. I want to bring about an eternal darkness, and it all starts with you. Anyone who believes in your

God will soon believe in me. Get use to this, because you'll never see anything other than the darkness that surrounds you ever again!"

The beast grinned as the priest began to scream uncontrollably, trying in vain to break free from his restraints.

Chapter 26

Fr. Roche awoke early on the morning of Alan's funeral and climbed to his feet within the dark-filled bedroom. Rubbing his hand across the stubble growth on his face and stinking of sweat, he decided to have a shave and step into the shower before celebrating the Mass of the body he found days earlier.

Settling his shirt in the mirror, he snatched his coat and stepped into the bright sun kissed day. Making his way to the church, he scrunched his eyebrows and shook his head, not enjoying the beautiful scenery which surrounded him. Finding the holy building, he went inside.

As he walked up the aisle, he eyed the coffin, and the shiny cross screwed to its lid. Passing it, he rubbed his hand along the side of the casket and grinned. The priest paused momentarily at the altar, again grinning, and then stepped around and stood behind it. He slid his hands beneath the book proudly set upon it and studied the words. After reading for some time, he slammed the cover shut, then stood there taking in the statues and paintings around the fabulous building. His attention turned to the front door as the first of the mourners began to flow into the church.

"Morning, Father," the elderly lady said as she placed herself on the wooden pew.

"Morning, Mrs. Byrne. How are you?"

"No one has called me by my maiden name in quite some time. I didn't even think you knew it," she said, amused.

"I know a lot about the people around here, Mrs. Byrne. I've to go get ready to celebrate this Mass now."

"Okay, Father," she replied.

Following the Mass, they made their way out to the cemetery, located on the church grounds. A lot of people came to pay their respects, and they gathered around the six-foot deep hole in the ground. The priest recited some words of prayer which the mourners had never heard before. Mrs. Byrne, noticed that he held the prayer book upside down, but didn't want to highlight it due to the occasion, and she assumed that's why he was saying things like *"You're with me now.", "Alan now sees what awaits after death",* and *"He is with all the others."*

As the coffin was slowly lowered into the ground, individuals paid their respects with the remaining distant family and friends, and then made their way to a local pub where refreshments had been arranged.

The priest stood glaring into the hole as the last of the family members made their way back to their car.

"You'll never fucking rest in peace. I have you

now. Just like I have this pathetic fool. Soon, they'll all be mine!" He muttered towards the dead man's decaying body below.

"Are you joining us, Father?" Mrs. Byrne shouted back to him from the old, rust incrusted gate.

He turned towards her with a large out of place smile on his face and said, "Yes, don't worry. You're next on my list."

The End.

About the Author

Chris Rush lives in County Wicklow, Ireland. His goal is to make each story darker and more disturbing than the last. Being a huge fan of horror, he strives to find new ways to scare people, long after they've closed the cover.
www.chrisrushauthor.com

Other Books by Chris Rush

FOLKLORE
THE LEGEND OF LOFTUS HALL

13096134R10102

Printed in Great Britain
by Amazon